Creation
of the
Southern
Nation

The Memoirs of General-in-Chief
Thomas Jenkins Worth, CSA

Christopher G. Owen

ARCHWAY
PUBLISHING

Archway Publishing books may be ordered
through booksellers or by contacting:

Archway Publishing
1663 Liberty Drive
Bloomington, IN 47403
www.archwaypublishing.com
1 (888) 242-5904

ISBN: 978-1-4808-5131-3 (sc)
ISBN: 978-1-4808-5130-6 (e)

Library of Congress Control Number: 2017952729

Print information available on the last page.

Archway Publishing rev. date: 08/21/2017

This book is dedicated to Sue.

Contents

Foreword

With the issue of the War Between the States, or the Civil War, it is important to consider the possibility of a different outcome other than what took place. Historians have deemed the Battle of Gettysburg the "high-water mark" of the Confederacy. Had the Confederate Army won that battle, would that have led to overall victory, which for them meant the right to secede? General Lee himself said that he would have won that battle had Stonewall Jackson still been alive to participate. Given Jackson's track record of taking on and defeating numerically superior forces, there is much credibility to his statement.

This path to victory for the South that historians find credible was not, however, the only path. There was a very credible path to victory in the west also. A victory at Shiloh, which Albert Sidney Johnston very nearly achieved, could have presented the Southern war effort with a completely different array of possibilities. This fictional account considers those possibilities.

The Civil War was a massive outpouring and display of civic duty, one almost impossible to conceive happening today. The armies on both sides fought with a zeal and ferocity rarely seen in history. Civic duty may take many forms, but the most militarily important form is patriotism. Patriotism is the love of one's country to the point where a person is willing to lay down his or her life for the survival of the country. That kind of patriotism, we see in abundance in the Civil War. To produce that kind of love, a nation must endear itself to its citizens. This doesn't happen by decree but by the structure of a society itself.

An important aspect of this structure of society at the time of the Civil War that we need to look at if we are to account for the intensity and ferocity of the fighting is the fact that citizen soldiers, not army regulars, fought the war. At the beginning of the Civil War, the regular army was tiny, only a few thousand men, and headed by an ancient man in his seventies who couldn't even mount a horse. It was the states and localities that came up with their own fighting formations and sent them off to the national leaders to flesh out the armies to fight the war. This structure still exists in today's Guard and Reserve units. They are the direct descendants of this structure. The men in these formations had not only a sense of loyalty to the country but also a profound sense of loyalty to each other and the states and localities from which they came. Their sense of civic duty and patriotism from this structure produced an esprit de corps that became the psychological fuel for unprecedented fighting spirit within the armies. Civil War battlefields were compact areas of horrific slaughter where hand-to-hand fighting in close quarters was not uncommon. Only men with the highest morale could participate in such bloodbaths, and many did so over and over again.

The contrast to today's army is striking. In an

uncommon era where the country evidently has money to burn, the leadership has abandoned the citizen-soldier army model for a large standing army as its primary fighting force. The regular army dominates the military investment of the country. And although the Guard and Reserve system still exists and participates in all the country's wars, the regular army administrative structure looks down upon and spits upon the service of career Guard and Reserve soldiers. There is no other way to put it. What used to be the primary engine of the American war machine due to its superior patriotism, today's military planners have marginalized in every way possible. Army Reserve outfits today are support units only, the planners having stripped all of the combat arms formations away two decades ago. Guard combat arms outfits still exist but at a low priority in equipment and training. They are set up to be thrown into the breech as cannon fodder, as happened in the Korean War due to a serious demobilization after World War II.

To give you a good example of what I mean about today's military structure spitting upon the service of the Guard and Reserve soldier, consider the following: An enlistee in the regular army can stay in a barracks for two years; have the taxpayer pay for his or her lodging, three square meals a day, medical needs, and pay; and at the end of a two-year period attain full veteran status with the Veterans Administration. A Guard and Reservist enlistee, on the other hand, has to spend twenty years in service, all that time providing for his or her own meals, lodging, medical needs, and pay, to attain the same full veteran status with the VA. And this is only a recent development within the last year. Before Congress passed this law, it was not unusual to find among the muster rolls of the Guard and Reserve system sergeant majors with thirty to thirty-five years' experience—literally thousands of meaningless "retirement points"—whom, after all those years of loyal watchfulness and commitment, the VA did not recognize as veterans. The truth is that they are the country's most patriotic soldiers. Who else would commit so much of their lives to a sacred cause, only for the system to give them a huge insult at the end of their careers?

Like the enlisted ranks, the vast bulk of the officer corps on both sides of the Civil War were citizen soldiers, not professional regulars. Moreover, the West Pointers who ran the Union Army for the first two years of the war led it from one disastrous defeat to another. It took a nebbish college teacher from Maine, who had no prior military experience but who was a naturally gifted tactician, to lead the Union Army to its first significant victory of the war. I am referring to Joshua Chamberlain, colonel of the Twentieth Maine Infantry, who learned how to be a soldier on the job and who invented tactics in his head that saved the Union left flank from collapsing at Gettysburg—not bad for a civilian in uniform.

I recently spent about six months in contact with Senator Angus King's office, trying to get his opinion as to what is the justification or rationale behind today's military administration's belittling or spitting upon the service of the Guard and Reserve soldiers, traditionally the nation's most patriotic fighters since the time of the minutemen. Ironically during this period, Senator King, as a civilian, received a prestigious medal from the US Navy while standing before a painting of Joshua Chamberlain charging the enemy with drawn sword. I finally did hear from the good Senator. He felt that it was not necessary to elevate the Guard and Reserve to veteran status. Moreover, he did not feel that it was important that they be able to celebrate the bloodless victory of the Cold War over a beer at an American Legion hall with other comrades even though many had spent decades on the muster rolls of the military waiting for the call to combat. And it is not necessary to award them with a medal for such service. That might cost the government 30 dollars or so and that money the Congress can better use for the politicians to award each other medals which they do frequently, even though they haven't served a day in uniform or ever got their hands dirty digging a foxhole. And also the Congress has to pay for their solid gold health care plan that none of the rest of us have access to, but I digress. They assume that there will never be a shortage of patriotic souls willing to sign their lives away for the flag. Like volunteer fire personnel, why give them anything if they are willing to volunteer? This official policy is such shortsightedness as history proves!

The South also had brilliant citizen soldiers among the officer corps. Nathan Bedford Forrest joined the Confederate Army as a private, eventually becoming a lieutenant general by war's end. His performance was nothing less than brilliant and legendary. His title in history is forever "the Wizard of the Saddle." One of Jefferson Davis's biggest regrets of the war was that he did not give Forrest more authority sooner. One can only imagine what would have happened in the west had Forrest been in command, instead of the professional soldier Braxton Bragg, who turned out to be a dismal failure as a front commander.

The citizen-soldier army and its blueprint as a product of the states and localities will always be available to the war planners. But the planners must not assume that citizen soldiers' superior sense of patriotism is a well that will never run dry. As the country's politics and culture become ever more balkanized, held together only by money, that sense of patriotism declines. If the planners continue spitting on the sacrifices of their most patriotic recruits, they will find the ranks too thin to be much of a useful force and therefore will have to fall back on conscription. Conscription in a fragmented society is not profitable or politically feasible. One only has to look upon nation-states of the past that had to rely on mercenaries and conscripts for their war-fighting capabilities. Mercenaries make inferior soldiers because they have little or no loyalty to the country that hires them. And once the money runs out, so does their service. The war planners would do themselves and the country a great service by expanding the Guard and Reserve and putting them on equal footing with the regular military forces, treating both as equals in recognition and prestige. Such a move would also be a practical check on the balkanization of the country into regions, seeing that federal authority would extend to them in the form of federal soldiers and federalized state soldiers. Such a policy would work to preserve national peace and help to ensure that another civil war on American soil could never take place.

Chapter 1

Beginnings: Mexico and Texas

Greetings to all of you who read this book! I am retired general-in-chief Thomas Jenkins Worth, CSA, and these are my reminiscences of the great war between the states that gave birth to our Southern Nation.

My father was Major General William Jenkins Worth, the liberator of Mexico. His efforts delivered the country to the United States, not the efforts of foppish General Winfield Scott, who took full credit for the genius and martial efforts of my father. My dad was a big-picture thinker and thought that Mexico could not thrive on its own and needed to be assimilated into the great democratic experiment that was his country. He served up Mexico by the sweep of his victories and handed the country to the Congress, who refused such a gift.

It was in his army where I got my start and saw the elephant. I quickly became a big-picture soldier myself. While my father went from point to point, smashing the Mexican Army wholesale, I concentrated on the little battles.

My classmate Thomas Jackson and I made our cannons sing a song of defiance and death to the enemy. I wasn't much for the cavalry. Though I loved horses, being a big-picture man, I realized that wars were not won by lightly armed cavalry, but by the main bodies of infantry backed by their crew-served weaponry. I was fascinated by the advancements in weaponry that were the products of science. The rifling of cannons and infantry guns, the use of percussion caps, and the prospect of rapid-fire weapons—all of these were greatly changing tactics of warfare, which evolved right before my eyes. I was determined not only to use them but to produce them myself. I studied metallurgy and different alloys with their varying bursting pressures. I could see that good old bronze and cast-iron cannons were rapidly on their way out. Whether or not this would take place in my lifetime, I was not sure. But smart men were making better weapons all the time, more accurate, with more rounds per minute, and with greater lethality and explosive force. Meanwhile, our tactics hadn't changed much from the old Roman style and the phalanx. We still massed men together in rigid Roman formations. The only difference was that in place of maintenance of formation and discipline with the new rifled muskets, discipline quickly faded, and all hell broke loose. Then instead of a rigid strike, you got a chaotic brawl. Three, four, or more strikes had to do what one charge of the phalanx used to do to seize an objective. But I wish to talk more about weaponry and tactics later.

I am sure people wonder about my own motivations in the war. Why would a lad from a Yankee family, born and bred in that tradition, want to throw it all away and fight for the South against his own motherland? Well, I have a whole host of reasons. For one thing, I befriended many people from the South and was stationed in Texas at the time of Sumter. These people became more than friends; they were like beloved family. The people of the South were enchanting in their manners and their way of life. Their lilting way of speaking was so warm, gracious, and courteous. I loved them dearly and could not think of even raising my hand against them.

And as far as the political causes of the war were concerned, it was unthinkable that they had to be settled on a battlefield and not in a court chamber or a legislature. The war was caused by a handful of zealots on both sides. There were insatiable fanatics with no compromise in them on one side versus greedy overseers and speculators on the other.

Most men whom I commanded and fought alongside had no use for slaves or connections with the institution. As a matter of fact, you had to look high and low to find such a person. Nathan Bedford Forrest was, of course, the big exception. The problem with slavery was the cotton gin. The prospect of quick money led to wholesale abuse of the slave folk. Most of us generals, above and beyond pure military considerations, agreed it was a strategic error, and most of us, if not all, were painfully aware of the intrinsic wrongness of it. But we were classically trained. We had studied the ancient wars and the ancient societies. We saw that the glory of Rome and Egypt had been built on the backs of slaves. It hadn't sunk in yet that the time of the greatness of Rome and Egypt had passed from this planet, never to be re-emulated. The South was not Rome, and the Southerners were not

Romans. The age of the modern world would not allow it. This was the age of full-page graphic depictions in *Harper's Weekly*—the plight of the Southern slave laboring away in the hot Southern sun, feeding the satanic contrivance known as the cotton gin with its unfeeling insatiability. Even the tzar of Russia had conceded that emancipating his serfs was the way for his society to survive in the modern world. To hang on to the institution of slavery and not phase it out as quickly as possible was insane for a society based on the equality of all men. Nevertheless, the majority of the Southern slaves maintained their loyalty, no matter the wrongs perpetrated against them.

But the North wasn't interested in freeing the slaves. The South wanted to handle the slave issue on its own and in its own good time. It was the zealots and the political demagogues who created the fear that Southern society would be taken over and destroyed. The zealots took the issue out of the courts and halls of the legislatures and onto the streets, where blood began to pour. Once blood was shed, the sides became hardened and uncompromising. This led straight to secession.

Like I said, the North didn't care about the slave issue. They cared only about the money that the South paid in tariffs to export its cotton. Lincoln once said that without the South as part of the Union, how was he to pay for the government? The violence brought on by the abolitionist zealots created a crisis situation that led to secession. And once secession happened, war became a certainty.

I didn't agree with the rush to war or the reasons behind it. It was unnecessary. For one thing, secession was not unconstitutional at that time. It was more than covered by the Declaration of Independence and the Tenth Amendment to the Constitution. Secession had never been decided upon in the courts. There was no legal precedent for it. The Constitution was our societal contract, and like any other contract, it was legally binding. If the terms of the old contract were no longer sufficient, then it was time for a new contract. But the government must first honor the terms of its original contract.

As far as financing the Northern government with the tariffs from the export of cotton, how hypocritical can you be? If the North was really so morally superior to the South, then they would have refused to take that money, knowing how it was produced—on the whipped backs of the slaves. But like I said, the North really didn't care about the slaves and would accept their blood money. And they had the gall to use the issue of slavery against the South as propaganda to undermine the interests of the South. Political leadership told the Northern military that they were fighting to free the slaves so that they wouldn't hesitate to invade and devastate the South.

The Southern Nation was a great nation that its founders painstakingly built. It was a grand and beautiful place, a horn of plenty, a graceful, civilized place full of pride in its creation. It was up to our generation to fix what was wrong in it and to not see it destroyed. For these reasons, I pledged my sword to its cause. The issue of slavery needed to be settled by the government and in the halls of the legislature, not by wild fanatics in the streets or in faraway, filthy, blood-soaked battlefields. I looked upon the Northern aggression against the South the same way I look on the sin of Cain against his brother Abel.

It is interesting to me to consider the religious aspects of the war. Zealots on both sides, as it often happens in war, declared God to be on their side. They had good reason to think so. Many pious men of the South considered it their mission to spread the gospel to the world. The question of slavery was secondary to all that. Were there not slaves in the Bible? The pious men of the North insisted that slavery, not the Bible, was the most important issue, and they had to handle it immediately. Many of the new cult of spiritualists talked about the divine spark within all human beings. I found their philosophy interesting and agreed with it to a great extent. My perception was that the Bible was such a porous document that just about any cause could find its fuel and legitimacy contained within its pages. *Forget about the book*, I thought. *Go out and see the people. Look into their eyes, and what do you see?* I saw a human being trying to make a living and keep his family together. Whether it was the slave or the poor Southern farmer, you saw the same thing. So it seemed that instead of spending our few precious years of life fighting with each other and oppressing one another, why not cooperate in a calm, deliberate manner and recognize what's good about each other and find that divine spark? But instead we had to settle the issue with armies. Once the armies in the field took over, there would be no end to the apocalyptic catastrophe of the two sides, whole societies, embraced in a death grip. This is what the zealots did not choose to understand. The Kansas-Nebraska Act led to Bleeding Kansas. Bleeding Kansas led to secession. Secession led to full-scale annihilation of one side or the other.

All of my family were universally disappointed in me and my subsequent decision to resign my commission in the US Army and accept a commission with the Southern army. I lost speaking terms with just about all of them, including my younger brother William, who ended up fighting for the North. However, I considered my adopted home to be Texas. It was where my father died and where I chose to carry on his legacy. I was born at West Point on October 5, 1824, when my father served there as commandant of cadets. And as a child I knew that someday I would graduate from the academy, which I did in the class of 1846. I graduated alongside my best friend, Thomas J. Jackson. We both went immediately to serve in the First US Artillery in the Mexican War. It was there that I learned how terrible war is and how events test a person's honor or lack thereof. I found that TJ was not just the kind, considerate dreamer that I knew and respected. He was also fearless and performed brilliantly under fire. I thought for sure he would be kicked out of the army for disobeying orders at Chapultepec Castle. But he saw the situation clearly in his mind's eye and knew he had gotten a bad order. His brilliance led us to a great victory.

But the greatest brilliance I witnessed in that war was that of my father. The Battle of Monterrey was his masterpiece because old Zachary Taylor, no-nonsense, kind, and generous as he was, gave my father a free hand to execute the battle. This was because Zack Taylor, God rest his soul, was a true selfless patriot who loved his country greatly. He felt that if everyone was allowed to do his job unselfishly, then there would be enough glory for everyone after the victory was won.

The atmosphere changed abruptly once General Winfield Scott took over command. My father had been fanatically loyal to the man starting with the War of 1812 and continuing all the way through to the Mexican War. My father even named my younger brother after him. He had my brother's name changed from Winfield Scott to William Scott after the scales fell from his eyes. General Scott ordered my father into every tough scrape and every bloodbath he could find up until the war's conclusion. The worst of these was Molino del Rey, when Scott acted on erroneous, untrue information about the existence of a Mexican cannon factory. He ordered my father to attack the position with his division. The position fell, and no factory was there. This cost the lives of over two hundred fine officers and men for no purpose whatsoever. The division had to absorb a full 10 percent loss of effective strength because Scott had failed to get confirmation on what was a baseless rumor. After the war concluded and Scott no longer needed my father's brilliant military mind to win his battles for him, he promptly placed him under arrest for insubordination—because my father had raised legitimate questions about his conduct. But I won't go into all the charges, countercharges, and courts of inquiry. I will end by saying that Scott showed who he really was as a person during this process—a vain, selfish popinjay of a man, a man with no generosity whatsoever and one who usurped all the glory for himself. As a soldier of the Southern army, of course, I was free to express these sentiments. I was not going to serve under such a man. My father died in Texas, and all the upset was forgotten. All the glory of that war fell in the lap of Scott, and my father's name would fade into the dust of time. My father would forever be the forgotten hero of the Mexican War.

As for myself, being the son of the general, I shunned every special treatment or consideration. My father had started in the army as a private and ended as the most brilliant and feared-by-the-enemy commander in the US Army. I knew that if I was to be a reflection of his light, I would have to assume as many personal hardships as possible. On nights when rations were short, I would give mine to my men. I never said no to extra duty. Exhaustion and fatigue became my friend and ever-present companion. I followed this path after the war and saw many strange sights at night. Sometimes I talked to the dead, and they would tell me things. Later on, when I served in the Department of Texas on patrols and made acquaintance with the Comanche medicine men, they would tell me that these dead men I saw were really alive in the spirit world. The spirits of the Comanche and the Apache actively gave information to the medicine men, which they used to lead the tribes in all things. This was all information that no Christian was supposed to listen to. But I guess I wasn't much of a Christian. If these spirits were alive, then where were heaven and hell? I found hell on the battlefield in Mexico.

Handling men under fire is a far different situation on the field than in the silent halls and classrooms of West Point. The stress that one feels at the loss of friends and comrades is inexplicable. It amazes me to hear people talk so nonchalantly about war. Such talk makes me angry. The only point of having a war is to get it over with as soon as possible. Overwhelming force and aggression are necessary for this to come about. Sometimes you have to create an evil in order to get rid of a greater evil. But the men whose bones lie in the dust of Mexico—where is their glory? You can remember so-and-so. He died with the army in Mexico. This is all we can say. And years later, people forget. They forget all too quickly the sacrifices that soldiers make. Where is the glory in that? The only thing that I remembered that was worth remembering is that victory is the result of quick, effective, well-planned action executed in the most violent way possible. Timing is everything. That I learned from my father, who never failed to steal a march when he had the opportunity.

After the Mexican War was over, I was assigned to my father's staff in the Department of Texas. A plague of cholera went through the Eighth Infantry Regiment at Camp Worth in late 1848, and in May 1849, my father, the most talented and gifted general of the war, died at his headquarters. Perhaps it was merciful that God took him. Certainly, the old fop Winfield Scott would have done everything in his power to sabotage his further career. I wondered about what the future would hold for me. I planned to bide my time and keep my own counsel and pray that I could fade into the countryside. So that's what I did. I stayed as far away from my dad's nemesis as possible, safe in Texas. And when I finally got my promotion to major, I felt that I was safe and that no one from the high command would bother me. And why would they bother me? The department was a vast frontier and at that time a very boring place. The excitement started during the Gold Rush and the cycle of negotiations with the Indian tribes to keep them peaceful, only for the waves of settlers to come along and sabotage the peace. These interlopers had no respect for the concerns of the indigenous inhabitants. Then fighting would break out, and the army would become the peacemakers again. I welcomed boredom. In the flare-ups of violence and the subsequent cooling-off periods, I got to know and respect the Comanche and Apache. The Comanche were the best horse cavalry fighters ever seen in the world. They compared only to what I have read in the history books about the prowess of the Mongolian horsemen of Genghis Khan. If the Comanche had lived in medieval Mongolia instead of the preindustrial United States, then they too might have conquered the known world.

The Apache, in addition to being great fighters, were uncanny in their spiritual gifts. They could see and talk to their spirit ancestors, who would tell them of the living and the dead. I would go on periodic patrols to the west into Apache country. In the course of these travels, my comrades and I would try our best to make friends and allies. I visited an Apache medicine man by the name of Gopan, which means "protector" in the dialect of his tribe. Gopan told me many things about the Apache god, spirits of the ancestors, and the spirit world in general. For Gopan it was all alive. There was nothing that was dead. People just transformed from one stage to the next in their existence here and beyond. Once they finished their work here, they moved to the next level of existence. But they still had contact with those who listened for them. Gopan warned me of the time to come, when rivers of blood would result from the evil that sprung from the hearts of some white men. He told me I would be very involved and to watch out for certain personages I would meet along the way. Gopan told me so many things about myself that were true that I did not doubt his premonitions. He told me that my dad was still there standing beside me. Then he told me certain things that no one else knew about him besides myself. For instance, he always carried a silver dollar in his pocket—the same one. He gave it to me on his death bed. He was my protector in the ether and kept me from harm, from the place he now resided. Gopan and I became great friends over the times I would visit, usually spring and fall. He performed his ceremonies with me, sang his sacred songs, and prayed to his friends in the ether about my success and protection. I was always uplifted by the man's presence and was regretful to leave when the time came to say good-bye to him and his shining wisdom. One might say that he was my spiritual teacher, and I was his student.

I took heed of his warnings of the future. One did not have to consult the spirits about the tremors and breakdowns occurring within the country. It was in the mid-1850s that the arguments broke out into brawls. And the brawls led to bloody violence. It was all the result of weak statesmanship, leadership at the top, and the corrupting influence of money and greed. The irresponsible weakness of the politicians turned what used to be a nation into a boiling cauldron of demagogues and demagoguery. And all I could think of was the line from Macbeth, "by the pricking of my thumbs, something wicked this way comes." Men beat each other with sticks even in the sacred halls of Congress. Discipline in any society is hard to achieve. Once achieved, it is hard to maintain. But once discipline, civility, and integrity are gone, society is lost and gone to the devil. The Missouri Compromise was the first mistake. It formally split the country into two countries, North and South. Gopan told me that this was like the rattlesnake being offended by its own tail. He would soon turn on it and try to eat it.

This is what indeed happened. The introduction of popular sovereignty broke the faith that the system could work. Southerners suddenly lost faith in the goodwill of their Northern brothers. They feared for their safety under the new system. They saw the killing of numerous whites in the Haitian Revolution and thought that the same thing could happen to them. They feared for their culture, their stability, their children, and their grandchildren. Abolitionists in the Northern governments and in the press began to rail against and curse them nonstop. The South became convinced that the snake had turned on its tail and was beginning to devour it. The North, on the other hand, allowed itself to be carried away with utopian notions that the whole slavery issue could just vanish over time with enough tongue lashings and pontifications pointed at the South, without any violence or bloodshed. The basic decency and goodness of the South, despite its failings, they smeared and dragged through the dust, using the power of abolitionist propaganda in the press. What the legal representatives of government could have and should have worked out peacefully in the halls of courts and legislatures instead moved out into the streets. Government rule handed over its authority to mob rule.

One of the abolitionist rabble-rousers to come forward was Abraham Lincoln, along with his new political party. He kept calling slavery a moral wrong, which of course it is. The question was turning a moral wrong into a legal wrong. That was where the danger lay. There were only two ways to accomplish this, peacefully over time or violently through waging war against one's neighbor. This, Lincoln would do by taking advantage of the firing on Fort Sumter. Lincoln could never get the moral-wrong aspect of slavery out of his mind long enough to engage in peaceful negotiation. It was this constant drumbeat of the moral wrong of slavery spewing from his mouth that eroded any trust and faith that the Southern people might have had in such a man. They became convinced that he meant nothing but the violent overthrow of their culture, way of life, and society wholesale.

The missing element in this calculus of destruction is the experience of the soldier. The burden in fighting in the event of war would fall on the backs of those veterans of the Mexican War. All the cadre of that war had experienced the gruesome nature of war and the changes coming about in arms and equipment. The strategic tactics had changed also. Napoleon had brought back to us the reality of total war in Europe. War was no longer a game of position in which you outflanked the enemy and he surrendered. Now it was all-out—country against country, population against population, generation against generation. Wars were no longer the affairs of noble knights in which the peasants were unaffected. Now all fought, from the lowliest peasant all the way to the scholars of academia and everyone in between. Modern war was no longer limited.

And in addition to the changed strategy, you had a whole list of breakthroughs in the technical contrivances of war. Not only could you count on the mass mobilization of the common man into the army, therefore swelling its ranks into a huge ocean of soldiery, but you also had railroads to transport them and their equipment, rations, and supplies. You had telegraph wires to coordinate logistics so that not only could you move the mass formations from a vast distance away, but also you could make sure that mass had food, equipment, and all its supplies already there when it got to its destination. The whole nation could now coordinate its resources and activities for warfare, on not a mathematical but a geometrical scale. Vast mobilizations on a never-before-seen scale were now possible. The war front could expand not just hundreds but thousands of miles across an entire continent. Navies that a short time prior had depended on the vagaries of sail and wind now maneuvered with the certitude of steam power and steam engines. Toss the sails away—who needs them?

So in the laps of that cadre of veterans from that nasty little war who had experienced its blood and horrors firsthand, the politicians now placed the responsibility of carrying the burden of total war on an unheard-of scale. Many of us had hardly gotten over our nightmares from that previous war and were appalled by the prospect of this new one that we would fight at home. Many of us, unlike the politicians, knew that we could not avoid this war and that many of us and our friends would not survive unscathed, if we survived at all.

But the populace in those naive days of the 1850s and their politicians had no vision of any such calculus as we had. They thought it all a lark to be over in just a few days, just like in the tales of the medieval knights and their limited skirmishes. "If there's a war, it will all be over in one battle"—that was the climate of opinion. This was the utter lunacy that we all had to argue against, and many of us did, at least until William T. Sherman was committed to a sanitarium for speaking the truth. By then it was time to shut up.

There was no way to effectively communicate that truth. Both sides derided any talk of impending cataclysm. Realism was defeatism on both sides of the Mason–Dixon. Nothing would overcome the fear of the Southerners that Bleeding Kansas would spread to become bleeding Alabama, Mississippi, Georgia, or South Carolina. Southerners had no prospect on the horizon other than a growing sense of chaos and anarchy. This, the election of the new president in Washington, fostered and encouraged those feelings of rebellion. That the new president would inevitably seek to undermine Southern society was a prospect Southerners would not tolerate. The Constitution did not expressly forbid secession. Indeed, the Declaration of Independence stated that it was the right and duty of the people to throw off a tyrannical government. And the Tenth Amendment to the Constitution buttressed the power of the states to be sovereign in everything not expressly given over to the federal government. Secession seemed to be the only logical way out of the dilemma. To Lincoln, of course, this not only was illogical; it could not be allowed to stand. How would I pay for the government, he said, without the revenues from the cotton trade? The greed for cotton money started and exacerbated the abuse of the slaves on a new scale. Now the loss of that money was the most important reason the North had to go to war. Only Homer could conceive of such a tragedy.

On a purely selfish note, the war would finally allow me to get out from under that dark cloud that hung over my career. General Winfield Scott would no longer be in my chain of command. At last I would be free of the general who had exploited my father's genius, laid claim to his hard-fought victories, and attempted to smear his good name and honor. Good riddance to that vain, bulbous popinjay of a man. Let the North have him, even though he can't mount a horse! Now I could be free to venture off of the frontier and not have to worry about keeping as much distance as possible between myself and Washington. It was not that I minded the boredom of barracks life in the Department of Texas, but it was nice to have the option of feeling safe in my own country again, as far as my livelihood and career were concerned.

I managed to keep a sharp eye out on the situation developing between the two soon-to-be adversaries during my time out west. Gopan told me that there were many new stars on the horizon. I kept looking for new developments in ordnance and tactics, in order to exploit those new developments. I found two that were especially interesting. I heard of a gentleman in England who had combined various chemicals together that could produce massive clouds of thick, persistent smoke. *What a wonderful way to mask and control movements on a battlefield*, I immediately thought. You could mask the movement of an offensive formation until it was too late to defend against them. The second was the development of metallic cartridges. No more cooling and charging and priming of ammunition. One could do it all cleanly and efficiently and, most important, rapidly with a metallic cartridge. I made my own mechanical drawings for rifles and cannons using the metallic cartridge. I placed a high value on seizing the initiative on these new developments, knowing that generals tend to stick with what they know and are slow to incorporate anything new until someone else proves it viable. The fact that the South was an agrarian economy and not industrial also led me to believe that these new technologies in weaponry would be critical to a Southern army's survival.

A Masonic brother of mine who had ties to the South, Richard Gatling, was a renowned inventor. I had personal discussions with him during furloughs that I took to Missouri in the 1850s. He showed me the plans for his new rapid-fire gun that could fire about four hundred rounds a minute. I had heard of the development of repeating rifles, but a weapon like this could have devastating effects that could change the course of a battle. He claimed he would have working models no later than the summer of 1860. I studied and postulated the potential effects of the employment of not just one but a battery of several of these weapons. I figured that with as few as six of these weapons, which our artillerymen would place in strategic positions or on high ground, the effect could reduce a corps-sized formation in the open field to a 50 percent casualty rate in as little as fifteen to twenty minutes. The first five minutes of such a battle, the artillerymen would use to find range and knock out opposing artillery in counter-fire operations. Once they neutralized that threat, then they could focus on the main body, and nothing the enemy could do would stop its annihilation. Enemy artillery gunners would not be able to employ their weapons once the Gatling gunners found their range. A barrage of interlocking rapid fire would make the cumbersome drill of servicing a cannon impossible. These weapons on the battlefield would have the impact of a giant scythe cutting down row after row of soldiery on the march, like rows of wheat shafts. I decided to secretly develop the weapon myself with the permission of Gatling, with his design and a team of gunsmiths and armorers.

I knew the army like the back of my hand. All armies move slowly like giant elephants. It takes a quick mind to innovate on the battlefield. Regarding just these two innovations, smoke and rapid fire, no one had yet conceived of or written the tactics that would make these weapons win battles and wars. Enemy battlefield commanders would be dumbfounded and overwhelmed when our soldiers employed them. These were two trump cards that I kept hidden in my vest pocket. The day would soon arrive when I put them on the table.

The political climate in the late 1850s continued to deteriorate at an ever-accelerating rate. Propaganda from the abolitionist activists continued at a high fever pitch in an ever-inflammatory tone. There was no compromise with such a din of extremism—no solution other than war and the pouring out onto the ground rivers of soldiers' blood. The only thing a Southerner could say complimentary to Harriet Beecher Stowe's work was that at least she depicted Simon Legree as a Northerner. Such inflammatory literature and political rhetoric, coupled with the greater need for slave labor to feed the cotton gins and the resulting abuses of the slaves, created a highly explosive political atmosphere. The gunpowder keg was full of dry powder, and the man who lit the fuse was John Brown.

My own political solution at that time was to have the US government divert some of those sacks of tariff cash that it collected to put up a practical solution. Waves of foreign immigrants from Europe packed Northern cities and languished without adequate employment. They never went to the Southern states. Perhaps if Washington had decided to provide work incentives for these deprived masses to come down South, work on the plantations for pay, and take the enormous pressure off of the slaves, that would have been for the good of the country. Perhaps if Washington had used the stacks of cash it collected to buy freedom for the slaves in the fields and make them productive farmers, this too would have been a solution, or a help anyway. But no such innovative solutions ever had been forthcoming from Washington or ever would be. All that came from Washington was threats of war, mobilizations, and plans for invasion or the strangulation of the South by a US Navy blockade in the event of secession. The latter idea came from the old fop General Scott himself. He knew he wasn't going to be the one out there enforcing it.

In my mind and in the minds of the cadre of soldiers, anything was preferable to war. The people promoting war, the firebrands and warmongers who had never experienced war for themselves, were like children playing with a loaded gun. The Mexican War veterans had seen the unseeable and heard the unhearable that is war—things that no one should ever have to experience. We had seen enough of our comrades and friends butchered and heard the horrific groans of the dying. We had seen the bullet-torn heads, the splattered and hanging entrails. I had witnessed it all down in Mexico and was horrified that this prospect was now hanging over our country and the people I knew and loved. As I said earlier, the only point in war is to get it over with as soon as possible. In this nationwide tragedy, it was ironic that those who knew what was coming were the ones the masses chose to ignore. But yet when the time came, those masses who thirsted for war would turn to us to show them the way to their own slaughter and death. And in order for us to limit the slaughter, we would have to embrace death for all its worth and become experts at dishing out death on a mass scale, in order to extinguish it as quickly as we could.

I wrote correspondences to old TJ. He had ensconced himself at some military school in the South. We discussed how the war would be and our chances for victory or even survival. TJ and I had developed a friendship that only comrades in battle could understand. It encompassed absolute honesty. We had learned to cope with the horrors we lived with in our own ways. TJ sought refuge in his religious beliefs that he had acquired during combat. These convictions had grown with each boom of the cannon. We both learned the pointlessness of fear. All fear would do is sap one's strength and cloud the mind. Only one route led you to survival and the preservation of your honor, and that was total commitment to your duty. Only through that narrow doorway in your mind could you silence the ferocity of the enemy guns. Only through that narrow passage could you preserve life another day, yours and your comrades'. And the ultimate goal was victory. What was victory? It was silence of the guns. It was preservation of self and honor. It was preserving the lives and honor of others with you. I wrote many letters over the years to TJ, and he addressed every one of my concerns, usually referring to some verse in the Bible. I did not rely on Bible verses for my inspiration. TJ knew that, but it never perturbed him. My strength came from the example my father had set. It was that standard that I tried to live up to every day. I felt that if I was half the soldier that he was, then I would prove a mighty asset to any military organization.

In several letters, as the political situation in the country deteriorated, TJ and I corresponded about the prospects for a Southern army versus the North. We both knew the prospects were bleak. Assuming that the authorities would not allow us to use slave soldiery, then the disadvantage in manpower would be roughly four to one against us. The disadvantages in logistics were even worse. Without the state of Virginia entering the war, the South would not have a single munitions factory capable of manufacturing artillery pieces. The South was a vast stretch of farms and plantations devoid of factories necessary to produce what an army needed to wage war in the field. It had little ability to support large armies. Indeed, the war would be a great bluff with a poor poker hand at the start. The North would start with a hand of aces in this regard, the South with deuces. The South would need time to put together even the minimal resources for war fighting. And with the deteriorating political situation, neither of us thought we would have that time to build before hostilities broke out. We would have successes at first under superior leadership, but once the war of attrition set in, the Northern juggernaut would prevail. Once hostilities broke out, I asked TJ, how much time would we have to achieve victory? One year, he replied, not much more than that. We had to achieve victory within approximately a year, or the effort would fail. It was all a mathematical equation. "We are a lion in the forest," TJ said, "but we are a lion fighting a bull elephant. Our only chance is to jump on the elephant's back and pierce its neck with our fangs in hopes that once it bleeds enough, it will turn tail and run away." This was all we could hope for because never in history had a lion slain a bull elephant. And if the lion failed to get at the elephant's neck and fell, the elephant would certainly trample it underfoot and grind it into the dirt.

I started to preach against war like all my former comrades. But no one was listening. Likewise, both TJ and I said that once the war became inevitable, we would preach for total war, and no one would listen. There was a strange aspect to the Southern gentry that I had observed acutely once I became immersed into their society. As a Northerner, I noticed the tendency of what I call misplaced chivalry. I will describe it as best as I can. A Southern gentlemen would never back down from a fight. But once he had hurt his adversary, it was not gentlemanly to hurt the adversary too badly. This cultural training was a straitjacket in modern war. It is a tactic fit only for storybooks about knights and their fair damsels. Those of us who studied Napoleon knew how fatal this noble sentiment was in modern times. TJ and I were free of this programming because we had learned war through experience. TJ's philosophy of war came from the Old Testament book of Joshua. He had no use for the tales of King Arthur. My philosophy came out of a love for the certainties of natural law and science. Neither of us was under any illusions about what the coming war meant.

As far as strategy was concerned, TJ came up with a pincer strategy in which two Southern armies, one in the west and one in the east, would invade the North at either end. They were to punch through the enemy lines and attack the interior of the country. The success of the pincers in a double lightning strike was, we figured, our only chance for victory. If the shock of the onslaught became too overwhelming for the enemy, then Lincoln would have to listen to overtures for peace. These armies would have to break away from their supply lines and would have to live off the supplies of the North. I also subscribed to this strategy of TJ's and considered it a prophecy. Such a strategy would test the Southern gentry's sense of chivalry to the utmost, but that would be the price of victory. TJ said to me several times, "We must show them the black flag." TJ wanted no quarter and would accept none in the true tradition of the ancient Israelites against the Philistines. I hoped that military necessity would stop short of that.

We both agreed that in order for the Southern armies to achieve victory, we would have to win every major battle with no exceptions. The first major loss, and the entire effort would unravel. But we also both agreed that although the North had the potential for an unlimited supply of new well-trained officers in their officer corps, the current Southern officer corps had the cream of the existing talent from the former US Army. In this lightning war that TJ and I conceived, quality would be necessary over quantity.

I don't know why TJ and I thought so much alike about warfare in general and the upcoming war specifically. He gave all the credit and insight that he had to God. I had found that my insights were coming to me from a divine place also, but I believed that some of my inspiration was coming from spirits who had passed—people whom I had known, soldiers, family, friends who would make their opinions known to me in dreams or momentary visions. It took my friendship with Gopan to make me realize that this was normal. When I feel the presence of my father, it's because he's there next to me, in the spirit world. Of course, I never told any of this to TJ. He was such a pious man that I could not and would not say anything that might jeopardize our friendship, especially now. I relayed information to him that I felt was coming from spirits. But I had to phrase it very carefully. I would say that I felt the presence of an angel of God warning me of such-and-such. Or I would say that I felt that the hand of God had touched me and I had received this message or something to that effect. The truth is that when the spirits of the dead came to me with information, the events that they predicted in that information came to fruition without fail. Before my father got cholera in Texas, for instance, I had a vision of him reviewing and inspecting the soldiers of the Mexican War. The important aspect was that I noticed that these were all soldiers who had died, every one. I knew at that moment that my father would be dead soon, although I didn't yet know the cause. He died of cholera within the month.

The information that I was getting from Gopan buttressed the messages I myself had received from spirits. As far as the coming war was concerned, I was completely psychologically, emotionally, and physically prepared by the time it finally happened, thanks to the warnings that spirits had given me. I had a complete battle plan to execute, tactically and technically, that I would deploy from day one of the war. And TJ had one that he had formulated too, only his information came from the high angels of Almighty God, of course.

The interwar years came and went mostly in the barracks, but with some extended patrolling. In the year 1859, I had become saddle-sore from extensive travel to the New Mexico territories and in the North in the Comanche lands. My mission was more diplomatic than military, and I liked it that way. I had no wife or children, and I liked this that way also. I was married to the army. I couldn't see raising a family in one of these rough, desolate, stifling-hot posts. It wasn't the same for my father, who had taught at the campus of West Point back east, where life was more hospitable.

I visited with Gopan and told him I was not sure how much longer I would be in the Department of Texas. He told me that I would be gone for a long time but that we would meet again someday. I asked him if he could see anything from spirits for me or the people of the South. He said our destiny was up to us. He also said that along the journey of war, I would meet up with a badger and a fox among the enemy. I was to take them prisoner and never let them free. If I did that, all would be well.

I sent letters to TJ on other issues regarding the debacle of impending war, not just military issues. I made it clear that we had to take the issue of slavery out of the hands of the politicians and the money interests. The problem was the abuse of slaves brought about by the need to feed the cotton gins and the corruption of society toward greed that the money men brought about. These money men were a combination of opportunists from the South with questionable morality and those who swept down from the North like vultures looking for a quick feast of money. The third player in this tragic drama was the federal government of the United States, which loaded the coffers of the Department of the Treasury with cotton money on the backs of the slaves. We could not expose another generation of Southern children to the disgraceful example of this situation. We needed reform of this situation on our terms from within, but reform must and would come one way or another. I knew that we must remove this defect in our society so that our children and the grandchildren could hold their heads up high and have the respect of the children of other countries. Slavery had to come to a quick end, the sooner the better. We would have to put down the politicians and the money interests with a military government, if necessary, but one the Southern officers would lead, backed up by Southern soldiery, not invaders from the North.

TJ always responded positively to these sentiments. He had communicated with Southern officers and found them in agreement. This reliance on slave labor to sustain the cotton economy was immoral, unchristian, and in his words the work of Satan himself. If we were to make the supreme commitment to war, then the institution would have to come to an end. Both of us believed that soldiers' blood was about to pour in rivers from one end of the country to the other in a massive war. Only the politicians and the press were naive enough to believe that it would all be over in a day.

The year 1859 continued, and the troubles continued to wax over the country. Then, in mid-October, came the insurrection that made John Brown famous. He tried to create an armed slave revolution—just what every Southerner had feared. He was a madman, of course, and had no idea what he was doing. Colonel Robert E. Lee, an acquaintance of mine and fellow comrade of the Mexican War, captured him.

Then followed the year 1860, which was a presidential election year. We saw the rise of the new abolitionist political party whose members called themselves "Republicans," a party led by a tall, lanky rail-splitter and homespun lawyer from Kentucky by the name of Lincoln. During the election, the Democrat Party split under two leaders. This allowed the upstart party to squeeze through and get control of the presidency with the support of not a single Southern state.

The politicians in South Carolina warned that the state would secede from the Union if Lincoln got elected. Some Northern folk asked me why South Carolina seemed the most radical of the Southern states. I have always said that it was all about money. Their politicians seemed to take the cotton tariffs most seriously. They had even voted not to pay them once, which was a law that the federals quickly overruled.

South Carolina followed through with its threat three months after the election, followed by six other states in rapid succession, including my very own Department of Texas. Once again, South Carolina seemed hell-bent on driving the issue toward war in the matter of Fort Sumter. The newly elected president of the Confederacy's government thought it prudent to push the issue. I had known Jefferson Davis personally as a military man in the Mexican War. He had worked closely with my father in the occupation of Mexico City. We were on good terms, and that would work to my advantage now that he was my boss. He was a very noble gentleman, which troubled me somewhat. He came straight out of the mold of the Southern gentry that I earlier described—those who adhered to the code of misplaced chivalry. I thought the move against Sumter was a terrible mistake. The proud seven states that had thus far seceded were in no way prepared to wage war against the Goliath of the North. Such a notion seemed lunatic to many military men of the day. I am not sure why Mr. Davis would do such a thing as fire the first shot, unless he was goaded by other noble gentlemen like himself. It made absolutely no sense to any of us. I likewise knew P. T. Beauregard. When

I first got the news of the firing on Fort Sumter, I wondered if Old Bory had lost his mind. But of course, he was only following orders from Jeff Davis. *A shame*, I thought. *God save us!* I heard of the fit Tecumseh Sherman had when he heard the news. He told his Southern friends that there was no way the South would win the war. I had to agree with him. Certainly, the seven states that initiated the war had committed suicide but had no way of knowing that yet. Robert Toombs said it was suicide, and he was right. The Southern states could have tied up the issue of the legality of secession in the courts for years and might have even won the case. The Supreme Court had been favorable to the South in its decisions regarding slavery. This could have bought time to build up and properly outfit an army and make a more detailed defensive plan. The seven states, however, had no plan, no provisions for war fighting whatsoever. I'm surprised they could even come up with the powder it took to make Fort Sumter surrender. Tecumseh Sherman summed up the situation in a typical logical manner of speech that I had heard from him before: "You people of the South don't know what you are doing. This country will be drenched in blood, and God only knows how it will end. It is folly, madness, a crime against civilization! You people speak so lightly of war; you don't know what you are talking about. War is a terrible thing!"

Jeff Davis, now our president, certainly knew intimately every word of this truth coming from Sherman. He had been a brother officer and was a seasoned military man. Being out on the frontier, I was happy with anonymity, but I was out of touch with a lot of things. Davis must have been under a tremendous amount of pressure from the radical secessionists in order to have precipitated the war so quickly. He was a responsible man and must have had a grasp on the fact that the South was so totally outmatched. But he made his decision, and war was what he chose.

The rail-splitter Lincoln, who had hardly had a chance to settle into his new surroundings after sneaking into Washington so that no one would recognize him, had his cause for war right in his lap. He wasted no time in taking full advantage of the gift. The Northern politicians, almost as naive as their counterparts in the South, were stepping over each other in pledging themselves and the lives of the male citizenry to participation in the upcoming bloodbath. Lincoln called up 75,000 soldiers. He got pledges of that number and many more. This call-up triggered four more states to join the Confederacy. The most significant of these, of course, was Virginia. Not only did we finally get access to some military manufacturing facilities, but also some of the finest officers in the army would now join us. The military talent could shorten in some respects the terribly long odds against us. Our problems remained, however. The two greatest were the North's four-to-one advantage in manpower among men of military age and our lack of an industrial manufacturing base. The state of Massachusetts alone had an industrial base over one and a half times greater than the entire Confederacy.

In my correspondence with TJ, we both agreed we had no margin for error and could not afford to lose a single battle. Unfortunately, the surrender of Fort Sumter was a terrible strategic defeat. So our doctrine of no defeats and no room for error was even more pressing now.

This begins my own personal story and entry into the war. I had made my intentions to join the Southern forces known to my family back east some time ago. So it was no surprise to them when I gave them the news of my resignation of my commission. My younger brother decided to join the Union Army as a private to balance things and to restore the family honor. In January 1861, the army accepted my resignation. I was a free civilian for a very short time. If I had any common sense, I might have fled the country. But instead I offered my services to the Confederacy. I promptly received a colonelcy in the regular Confederate Army in Texas. It became my job to arrest or detain any soldiers who had decided to maintain their allegiance to the Union. This I did, and later in the year 1861, I helped to organize first one Texas regiment and then another. In the fall of that year, I got my promotion to brigadier general. Significant fighting in the west didn't come until August, with the Battle of Wilson's Creek.

Back east, TJ had covered himself with glory at the Battle of Manassas. He had a knack for finding advantage where no one else could find it. I was so proud of his performance and to be able to call him my good friend. So far the South had yet to experience defeat. These were two minor yet respectable victories. They were enough to plant the seed of doubt in the minds of the Northerners. Although they had the resources to dominate this war, perhaps they didn't have the stomach for it.

In January 1862 I was summoned to the Confederate

capital, now in Richmond. There I got a second promotion to major general. I expressed to President Davis my reservations about receiving three field-grade promotions over the course of a year when I had yet to fight in an engagement. He said to me, "Thomas, I witnessed what a brilliant commander your father was and how you learned your trade at the feet of the master. I have no doubt that you will bring us many victories. Things are working rapidly, and we will soon have large-scale fighting in both east and west. The time of preparation is over. The real test is about to begin."

It appeared that President Davis had not exaggerated in his declaration of the faith he had in me. I carried with me the aura of my father, it seems; his brilliant victory in Monterrey in the Mexican War was a source of legend among many of the old-timers in the army. My job was in the Trans-Mississippi area. The western bank of the Mississippi River needed to remain in Confederate hands, but Union forces were intent on driving Confederate forces out of Missouri and moving down to threaten Arkansas. The victors of the Wilson's Creek battle, Major General Sterling Price and Brigadier General Benjamin McCulloch, although they supported each other in victory, had soon become bitter enemies. Neither one had much respect for the other or the other's fighting units. In order to maintain harmony, President Davis appointed me to overall command. This was to happen on the eve of battle, just before a major clash with the invading Union forces.

Chapter 2

Pea Ridge

In the meantime I sought out old friends whom I hadn't seen in years, now that we wore a new uniform. They were in winter camps in Virginia, or so I thought. I wasn't sure exactly where TJ was. I heard it on good authority that he was maneuvering his brigades around northwestern Virginia. His wife, I found out, was staying in Winchester in the house of a Reverend James Graham. I felt that I would intercept him there. When I reached the town, I found that TJ had arrived there just a short time earlier himself. After I arrived at the household and made my greetings to TJ and everyone else, I rather bluntly said, "TJ, we have to talk."

"Indeed, we do," he said. "Please excuse us, Anna."

"So you are continuing your exploits where you left off in Mexico," I said. "When I read the reports of Manassas, I thought to myself, this is vintage TJ; this is Chapultepec. This is Mexico City. You haven't lost a step. And now the people of the North are going to have all hell to pay every time they set foot in old Virginia and meet up with Stonewall Jackson. This is your new name according to the papers."

"Well, you are quite wrong," he said. "I just telegraphed in my resignation from the army and requested my old job back at the institute," Jackson said.

"Whatever for?" I said. "You are the most famous general in the South right now. That is the most insane thing I have ever heard out of the mouth of a general."

"Well, Thomas, no general worth his salt can tolerate his subordinates going over his head or can function with an army to command. My subordinates have taken it upon themselves to complain about my orders to the office of the president himself, and I have just had my orders to invest Romney countermanded. If that is the lay of the land, then they obviously no longer need my services," he said in a quiet voice.

"TJ, you know that they will not accept your resignation. There is no way on God's earth that they would. This is so absurd. I don't even want to know the details. There is no time for such nonsense. I'll tell you what. The day you resign is the day that I resign, and then the war will be over for the South. Now let's talk about more substantial things. The whole North American continent—indeed the whole western world—is still abuzz about your great victory at Manassas Junction. I was too until I analyzed the details. And the most important detail was that there was no follow-on pursuit. This had nothing to do with you, but with high command. What happened to Old Bory in this? Without you, TJ, that battlefield would have turned into a more god-awful mess than it was. Do we have the capability to drive the enemy and pursue him or not?"

"In my opinion," Jackson said, "we do have that capability. The problem is that the high command has not analyzed the situation to the same extent that you and I have, with one exception. Robert E. Lee talks and thinks the same way you and I do. He knows that our time of opportunity is very limited. We talked about the time frame of a year. Well, that year is almost expired, and we are no closer to salvation for our country. I believe that once we get the right leadership among the officer corps, then the lower ranks will follow our lead, God willing."

"We must start talking more about this with our commanding generals, TJ. We have no time to waste, and you have always been, if you pardon me, a tight-lipped man. I hope you are expressing these ideas to both higher and lower ranks."

Jackson let out a rare laugh. "Yes, tight-lipped with everyone but you, in the vain hope that through my friendship you may find your peace with God."

"Now, now, please let's not bring God into this," I said. "I believe in God in my own way, which admittedly is not like yours. The god I am interested in at the moment is the god of battles. Keeping the laws of that god is what we must do now if we are to survive. Right now we have the political situation to worry about as well. But I believe now, having talked with you, that we can resolve this positively. We have to have the blessing of the president in everything we do. I believe we can have it. Jeff Davis is not a friend of Old Bory or Joe Johnston. He gets along very well with me, Lee, and

Sidney Johnston. Heck, I've gone from unknown, forgotten, dust-covered major to major general in a year's time without having yet fired a shot in anger. I am still riding on my father's reputation. But this shows the faith that Jeff Davis has in me, and by God, I am not going to disappoint him.

"I feel that the president needs to curb his likes and dislikes. I have always looked up to Old Bory and Joe Johnston as solid military leaders, even though I had some doubts after Manassas Junction, when they seemed uncoordinated. It was the junior officers like you who won that battle. I have unveiled my plan to Davis, which is a strategic pincer movement with the simultaneous invasion of the North by the western and eastern armies, but I am sure he is hearing about this from all the far-thinking officers— yourself, Beauregard, Sidney Johnston, and Lee. He seems strangely reticent about invading the North, and I don't understand why, other than it's the old Southern honor code again. It's okay to beat the heck out of the enemy on the field, but it's not okay to take the fight to the infrastructure that gives the enemy his fighting capabilities, for fear you may hurt innocent civilians. We have to convince him to discard this ancient moth-eaten belief, or not only will we not win this war, but we will not gain independence, and we will not survive as a country at all. We absolutely cannot sit here in the South and wait for them to attack us and make mistakes. This will devastate our infrastructure, leave our civilians open to attack and depredations, and solidify the battle of attrition that we both know we cannot win."

Jackson heard me out and then said, "Yes, I have been pressing for such a strategy also. I have not conceived of it in the west, however, but now I do see it. If we coordinate movements, one such invasion will support the other. I will spread the idea."

"Yes, and we will need to cut ties to our bases," I said. "The South's ability to support us is limited anyway, without our being a terrible hardship on our own civilians. Once we penetrate the soft underbelly of the North, to feed and equip our forces, we will have to confiscate whatever rations, forage for our horses, equipment, clothing, arms, and iron that we can from the Northern countryside and cities, without worrying about the consequences to our host. We need not to be asking how King Arthur and his knights would do this."

"What's that?" Jackson asked.

"You know, TJ, this misplaced chivalry that got us into this mess in the first place and only promises to bring us ultimate defeat."

"Oh yes, I understand what you mean."

"TJ," I said, "I swear to you, with you and God as my witnesses, once I have committed to the invasion of the North, I will not turn back under any circumstances and will disobey orders for recall if Davis makes them. But I have the feeling that once I put together a string of victories, Davis will not recall me. I am determined to show all the Southern gentlemen dreamers how this war has to be won. Circumstances force us to win this war on a shoestring, but having said that, we will confiscate Northern shoestrings too. And once I have this machine in motion and cross over into enemy territory, the Northern newspapers will shout so loud that they will have to send half the Northern army after me, or I will strike them. Either way, I will not forget about the brothers in the east, not for one minute."

TJ was amused by this burst of optimism about my own personal plan to win the war. He paused for a second and then said, "Beauregard also has voiced to me many of his own stratagems that I have had the patience to listen to. How are you so sure that yours will work, if you pardon this question?"

"I know I can trust you with my life," I said. "I followed you on a few of those suicidal artillery duels in Mexico, and somehow, due to some miracle, we are here to talk about it today. I never doubted your abilities, TJ. You have an aura about you that comes to life in the most desperate situations. Right now, I ask you to trust me. All of these years, I have been out on the frontier, but I have not been idle. It's not in my nature to sit back at my desk with my feet up, watching the phases of the moon pass as time goes by. I have been looking for new ways to fight wars because I know deep in my soul that's what God put me here to do. And I have found those new ways. The world is changing rapidly every day now. Those who aren't catching on with the future will eat the dust of the past. I trust only a handful of men with my secret weapons. I have kept up and expanded my studies in engineering, chemistry, and science that they introduced to us at the Point. I have developed weapons that the scientists and weapons makers actually know about, but no one has tried them before in battle; therefore, their implications are unknown. I have perfected three such weapons that I believe will revolutionize the battlefield. Two, I will use freely, and you will read about their effects in the newspapers. The third weapon is so awful that I will consider using it only as a last resort. Once I produce victories from these weapons, you will know the truth of what I say. This will lengthen the period of opportunity for us and bring us to our goal of invasion of the North much quicker. And our political leadership must not stand in the way of that invasion because our survival depends on it. That's the difference between me and the fantasies of Old Bory. Follow my path in the west, and you shall see.

"There is one question I have left for you, TJ," I said. "What are our prospects for putting slaves in uniform? We could cover losses and create corps upon corps of replacements."

He looked at me with impatient frustration. "Those prospects at this time do not look good," he said. "The Southern gentlemen will not hear of it at the moment. The generals and the ranks would welcome the extra hands, but the politicians will not."

"This could be the critical opportunity to heal the nation's spiritual wounds from the stain of slavery and to move forward together into the future, all races of Southerners, be they red, white, or black. What is the reasoning? I can't understand this!"

"There is a fear that slave formations might turn against us or not fight," TJ said. "There is also the question of honor for the Southern gentlemen, who believe it is beneath their dignity to conscript slaves into war. You are very well versed on that subject. Then there is the question of compensation. How is the poor Southern government to pay for the freedom of the slave soldiers? The slaveholders on the plantations will demand compensation, and the money just isn't there. The money isn't even there for the war effort."

"This is all nonsense!" I said. "God save us from these greedy, corrupt moneyed interests who are unwilling to make any sacrifices for their country in a time of dire distress. Don't they know that if we lose the war, they lose their slaves anyway and a whole lot worse? Don't they know that the time of filthy profits from the fortunes of the cotton gin and the wholesale abuse of the slaves is over? Damn them to hell!"

"Now, Thomas," TJ said, "some things are beyond our comprehension and must be left up to the mind of God. The Almighty will deal with them in His own good time. You have no right to throw out curses."

"Okay, TJ," I said. "I guess I resent having my fortune in any way connected with theirs. You seem to have a closer connection with the mind of God on this matter than I do. I will take your word for it that I can gain nothing from curses. Unfortunately, now it is time for me to leave. You have my plans for the west. I know that you will remember them, especially when they start to unfold for the world to see. We have a lot of hard fighting ahead of us now. Please extend my regrets to Anna and the Reverend for my abrupt intrusion and departure, but I had to talk to you before I left Virginia."

"I admire your confidence, Thomas. May God go with you in battle, my friend. I will say many prayers for your success!" Jackson said.

With that I left. It took me a week of travel before I got back to Texas. For the next month, I made preparations to assume command in the Trans-Mississippi. I consulted with my weapons smiths and armorers and gave them instructions for the movements ahead. In early February 1862 I started out at long last on my mission of war with a detachment of regulars, formerly US, now Confederate, and a humble wagon train overland on my way to Arkansas. Three weeks later, after a leisurely trip, we arrived in Pocahontas, approaching the forward edge of the battle area. I had not seen any of these soldiers or their leaders before. After a rousing salute of cannons to announce my presence, I had sent word via telegraph that I expected all formations to be concentrated in the area of the Boston Mountains when I arrived. Included in this formation were the army of General McCulloch, numbering 8,000 effectives; the army of General Price, including some 7,000 men; and a force of pro-Confederate Indians from the Indian Territories that General Albert Pike commanded, a brigade of about 2,000. So altogether my command numbered some 17,000 effectives. The opposing force was 11,000 to 12,000 strong under the command of a fellow West Pointer and Mexican War veteran, General Samuel Curtis.

Along the way here, I had received news of the disasters at Forts Henry and Donaldson at the hands of General Ulysses S. Grant. With each one of these setbacks, the Confederate window for potential victory was narrowed, which put the whole effort of the war in doubt. I was impressed with the pluck of one of the cavalry commanders who had refused to surrender after the commanding officer had surrendered him and his outfit. Nathan Bedford Forrest was his name. He had said he was there to fight and not to surrender his command and then promptly extracted them out. I looked forward to talking to this non–West Point officer who was so full of fighting spirit. His was the only ray of light to shine from these dismal failures.

Finally, in the beginning of March, my trains and detachment were set up at Pocahontas. I rode out on the third to take command of the new Army of the Trans-Mississippi, and I really got an eyeful during the inspection. Never had I seen such poorly clothed, poorly shod, disheveled ragamuffins for soldiers! *How can they fight like soldiers if they don't look like soldiers?* I thought. Price's men especially looked terrible, probably as a result of being chased out of Missouri. A substantial number of the men walked barefoot. Many were dressed in rags. Many used rope to hold up their britches. "When was the last time you had a bath?" I asked one of Price's men.

"We don't take baths out here in the winter, General. It's too damned cold!" he answered.

By God, this will not do, I thought. *After this engagement we are going to start looking like soldiers—eating, washing, and keeping ourselves like soldiers. That will take some work, but it is going to happen.*

I summoned the generals and their staffs for a council of war. "Gentlemen," I said, "this council of war is informational. I am not asking for anyone's opinion. I already have a plan and will be mapping it out and telling you what to expect. As far as the enemy position, he is digging in now at a strong defensive position on Sugar Creek, where he will continue to dig in today, March 6. We have reports from our scout patrols that he has lost a few regiments while getting into position. They are strung out in the countryside somewhere and will not get here in time to participate in the battle. So this means we currently have almost a two-to-one superiority and can come down upon him like a ton of bricks in a brick shower. I can guess that some of you think a frontal assault against such a well-fortified position is foolhardy, if not suicidal. I can assure you it isn't.

"You will find out shortly that I am a different kind of commander and employ very different techniques and approaches to the problem of winning a battle. You see those ten wagons over there that I had brought up from Texas? They are filled with a new kind of artillery ordnance. These shells have been specially designed with special chemical compounds that do nothing but produce massive amounts of thick smoke. We can mask any of our movements and assault. The enemy can't shoot at us or fight us if they can't see us. We have sixty cannons, and at sunrise tomorrow our cannons will be firing those smoke-producing shells all up and down the enemy line. After a bombardment of a half hour or so, the smoke will be so thick that the enemy soldiers will be unable to see their hands in front of their own faces. It is then that we will focus on one point in the line and launch an assault. You are to order your men to pour through that point. We will choose a point where the smoke is most sparse so that our men will be able to see whom they are fighting. There will be no flanking maneuvers, just a straight frontal assault until we make a breakthrough. Then we will pour through and flank both left and right portions of the line and flood the enemy's rear. We should be able to achieve a reverse double envelopment of the enemy's entire line. And I am ordering a silent approach. There is to be no shouting until you make hand-to-hand contact with the enemy. Is it understood? Are there questions? General Price?"

"What are our men to do tonight in preparation?"

"Your men and all the men are to turn in as early as they can get settled tonight. I know that they have eaten all their rations, so there is no food. But at least they can build fires, stay warm, and get as much sleep as possible. We know where the enemy is, so there is no need to send out extra patrols. Keep guard duty to a minimum. They won't be bothering us tonight. I order your men to get as much sleep as they can. We will need their clear eyes and as much energy as they can muster for the morning. Anything else? Thanks, gentlemen, and may we be celebrating a great victory for the South tomorrow! General Pike, may I have a word with you for a moment?"

As Generals Price and McCulloch left with their staffs, I took General Pike aside. "General Pike, I would wish your division to lead tomorrow's assault. Will you accept this task willingly?"

Pike's face lit up like a firefly. "General Worth, I can't think of a greater honor."

"Thank you, General. I would like to place you on the extreme left. The wind has been blowing from west to east. We will have fifty cannons firing smoke, covering the whole line, but we will also have ten cannons firing solid shot on the left to reduce the dug-in positions. I have prepared for a thirty-minute bombardment. After twenty minutes we will start to lift the barrage of smoke on the extreme left and will switch from solid to explosive shot. We will roll off the barrage as your men charge forward in their assault. Since this is the first time in known history that a smoke screen is being actively employed to cloak a formation's movement on a battlefield, we can't predict with certainty the results. However, I predict the results will be stunning. I predict that with 80 to 90 percent of the line unable to see the movement and the other 10 percent shell-shocked from a punishing array of artillery fire, your men will be able to rush the position with very little hazard from enemy fire. Once you break through the line, we will be pouring in other brigades for an exploitation. You will find yourself in the rear of the enemy line and will be in charge of the envelopment. Roll up that line just as fast as you can, General. Don't let them escape. We want to swallow them whole, lock, stock, and barrel.

"Price and McCulloch will stay with me as they peel off their brigades and attach them to your force in the rear. Once you have achieved your breakthrough, we will switch off the smoke ordnance to solid and explosive shot to support your roll-up of the flank from left to right. But there is something I would like to say to your men, which I leave it for you to say as their commander. To the men of the great Indian nations whom the enemy has dispossessed onto the so-called Indian Territories, there are two things I would like to mention. First, I have seen the red man fight in the west and can say that there are no more skillful, more fierce infantry and cavalry as they on the face of the planet. Second, let the men know that they are fighting their oppressors, the nation that herded them like animals onto strange grounds, not the grounds of their ancestors. Their oppressors have defiled and corrupted the sacred lands of their ancestors. This is their opportunity to rise up and strike a blow against their cruel, heartless enemy. Furthermore, even though I am sending them in under military formation, I leave the tactics up to them. They can use the white man's tactics or those of the red man. They are to be the judge. They are allowed to use their weapons of choice. If they choose to drop rifles and fight with tomahawk and knife, they are authorized to do so. I think the shock effect of two thousand Indians attacking through the smoke will seriously demoralize the enemy. I am hoping the encirclement will be complete by noon. Do you have any questions, General Pike?"

"Are my men authorized to dispense with their uniforms, sir?"

"Yes," I said, "by all means, your men are exempt from normal protocol. If they want to dress in the regalia of their ancestors and wear war paint, they are authorized. It might be a sight better than the rags they are wearing now anyway."

Pike replied with great enthusiasm, "General Worth, I can't thank you enough. I myself will be on the field wearing a full chief's bonnet."

"Good luck, General Pike. I will see you and your men at dawn."

At dawn on March 7, it was a gray and foggy morning. The generals ordered their men to stand to and form a line of battle an hour before daylight. The good night's sleep had revitalized the men even though there were no rations available for them in the morning. The sleep had helped take the edge off of the forced march they had made in the cold March winds before getting here. The truth is that I needed to seize that enemy supply train just to give the men of my corps a square meal. And I had plans for all the clothing and accoutrements of the enemy army. As for the commander, Samuel Curtis, he had a West Point background and much experience, but he was a bit past his prime and not ready for my bag of tricks. My smoke screen would neutralize the entire line of breastworks that his men had so vigorously constructed through the night while my men slept. The Union men were all probably exhausted and knew that no matter what they did, they still were outnumbered two to one. They were on higher ground, overlooking the creek, and this normally would bode well for them. But today we were fighting with a whole new tactic that promised to turn the page of military history. Their advantages would be of no use to them.

On the extreme left of our line was Pike, then Hebert, and then McCulloch. Next were Price's Missourians, then fellow Texans, Arkansans, and Louisianans, all arrayed in front of the well-fed, well-equipped enemy. The enemy soldiers, although they had the advantage of height, were on a flat plain. It would be easy to move around them. Our batteries were on the south side of the creek and had open fields of fire all the way up and down the line. The enemy, although well dug in, had no idea what we had planned for them. They saw our campfires and were expecting a frontal assault in the morning.

I had issued orders at 3:00 a.m. By 4:00 a.m., deployments were complete. At full light I ordered the firing to commence. A thick blanket of smoke enveloped the enemy line after the first five minutes. After ten minutes the smoke was so intense that a giant cloud started to waft up from the field. It was obvious that no command or control was possible on the enemy line. I ordered a lifting of the smoke ordnance on the extreme left because I was concerned it might interfere with the assault force. I also made an adjustment, ordering an additional ten cannons to break off from the smoke and switch to solid and explosive shot on the extreme left, which was now getting pounded. After the twenty-minute mark, I sent word to Pike to get his assault force ready for the execution order. Twenty-five minutes into the barrage, I gave the signal to initiate the charge. The smoke had tied up the enemy's counter-battery fire capability. No doubt, the crews could not serve or aim their cannons. The shots that the enemy randomly lobbed in our direction had no accuracy, and all went wild, shallow, or high. They were uncoordinated.

Pike's Indians ran toward the extreme left. Our artillery lifted its fire as they went in. The men chose not to charge in organized rows or ranks but made a wild dash en masse, carrying their weapons of choice. Most carried a rifle until they came within range, at which point they took a shot, threw the rifle down, and then brandished knives and tomahawks—usually a knife in one hand and a tomahawk in the other. Some dressed in loincloths and leggings and dispensed with their shirts and jackets despite the cold temperatures. They swarmed over the enemy breastworks like a cloud of angry hornets, shrieking the blood-chilling cries of their warrior ancestors. *By God, I am glad they are on our side*, I thought. I almost felt sorry for the shell-shocked men in those trenches.

Our artillery continued to rake the rest of the line with solid and explosive shot as well as smoke. I guessed that 80 percent of that enemy line was incapacitated and useless, not even a part of the battle anymore. The Union men had hunkered down in their trenches, waiting for guidance and direction that never came because their officers were in a total state of confusion. Fifteen minutes after contact on the line with the enemy, Pike sent word back that that part of the enemy line had collapsed. Quickly, I ordered Hebert and McCulloch to support Pike on the double-quick charge. Two gray brigades surged ahead, still under the masking protection of the smoke screen. They disappeared into the breach on the left. Fifteen minutes after that, I could hear intense firing coming from behind the enemy line. Leaderless men started to get up out of their breastworks and run off to their left. I ordered a lifting of all artillery and a general frontal charge by all units of the entire line. A mad rush followed. All units charged at the double-quick up the enemy's earthworks, in a solid wall of gray.

By this time, Pike's, McCulloch's, and Hebert's brigades had covered the rear escape routes, and those were no longer open. With the enemy completely exposed and out in the open, our formations had achieved the envelopment. Twenty minutes of intense rifle fire and hand-to-hand combat continued after the gray line overran the enemy's works. Then resistance withered. One group of the enemy after another surrendered. Word came back to my staff and then to me that our infantry had located and captured General

Curtis and the German general Sigel. We rode forward to demand their surrender and the surrender of their army.

As we rode up over the enemy's works, we saw groups of men clustered at various points. Rifle fire was now intermittent and sporadic and quickly subsiding in intensity. We went from group to group of numerous gray-clad soldiers surrounding disarmed enemy soldiers. We were unsure which group we were looking for. We went forward in this odyssey of victors and the vanquished until we heard a shout.

"General Worth, over here!" It was Pike sporting his Indian bonnet. With him was a group of his warriors and two Northern officers, one older-looking and hatless and another looking downcast, twisting his rather copious mustache. As we got into closer proximity, I could see the general's stars and his gray hair. Pike later told me that the general had earlier thrown his hat on the ground and stomped on it in a fit of anger.

"General Curtis, I believe?" I said.

"That's who I am, and that's who you've got," he groaned.

"I will accept your surrender and that of your men and get them paroled today. However, I cannot give them much to take with them. For one thing, they have plenty of food; my soldiers have none. My soldiers for the most part are in rags, with no footgear and not even belts to hold up their britches. Therefore, I am ordering an exchange of clothing and am confiscating any surplus clothing and footgear you have stored in your trains. Your soldiers have fine factory-made garments with overcoats, leather boots, and belts with shiny metal buckles. They are to give those up and exchange them with my soldiers who are in need; then they will be issued their parole passes and will be free to go. This is to start happening immediately."

General Curtis said, "Now I know personally about the saying 'to the winner go the spoils.'"

I ordered my adjutant to arrange the exchange and to break out the chlorine we had with us.

"But sir," he said, "I thought you were saving that for the artillery."

"Go ahead," I said. "We will find a resupply at a later time. Right now we need to get the men clothed, shod, deloused, and fed as well as we can as soon as possible. And one more thing—the men are to wear their belt buckles upside down. From now on, the US will be an SN. Instead of the United States, the engraving will stand for the Southern Nation. I don't want to see any US emblems out there. Please tell all the men."

For the next several days I supervised the distribution of the enemy supplies from the captured supply trains—not that the men needed to be told to distribute the supplies. They were grateful to finally get shoes, boots, and clothing so that they could fend off the March winds that came whipping through the area. I did have to order the men to delouse because as the soldier I had first talked to told me, it was too damned cold to take a bath. In the next few days, all the buckets and large pots we could muster, we used for the making of hot water. The men built raging fires where they could strip down and wash themselves and boil their clothes in relative comfort.

We weren't able to parole all the enemy on the seventh. It would take another day to arrange all the clothing exchanges and paroles. In all, the enemy casualties were close to three thousand, and ours under one thousand. We sent the enemy army north minus all their weapons, gear, cannons, and supply trains. We boiled as much clothing as we could in the time that we had. The clothing exchange turned both armies blue and gray. When the Northern men were ready, they took their paroles and made their way up to Kansas and freedom.

Two nights after the battle, an old friend whom I had lost came to me in a dream to warn me that in the North I would become a very hated leader of the Southern cause. A few days later the prophecy proved correct. The Southern papers were glowing over the victory. The *Charleston Mercury* headline was "Worth's Army Annihilates Yankee Invasion at Pea Ridge." The *Richmond Examiner* enthusiastically declared, "Worth Sweeps Yankee Army from the Field." At the same time Northern newspapers stated their version: "Worth Denounced as Butcher of Pea Ridge, Many Atrocities Committed." *Harper's Weekly* detailed the initial assault by Pike's Indians, claiming that they had scalped many Northern soldiers. The survivors of the battle were "stripped of their clothing and sent North naked against the winter elements with no supplies or food."

I was aware of some scalpings that had taken place and immediately put out an order forbidding the practice. But I did not press charges against any of Pike's men. Arkansas was Southern soil, part of the new Southern Nation, and the invading army had gotten what they deserved in my mind. And as to the clothing exchanges, if I had a choice between their men shivering and hungry in the winter cold or ours, then by God, it would be theirs. Though I regretted the desecration of the bodies of the Northern soldiers, this was something that green soldiers in their exuberance had done, not something that I had been able to predict ahead of time. All I could do was make every man understand that it was not to happen again.

I addressed the men on March 11 while awaiting orders. A wire arrived from Richmond thanking the men in the highest possible terms for their victory and their role in making the Trans-Mississippi free from enemy threat. I admonished the men to refit, rest, and prepare themselves for new orders for more action immediately ahead. Those orders came on the thirteenth.

In the meantime, I spent my time updating myself with details of other actions that had happened along the front— the fall of Fort Donelson in the middle of February and the Battle of Mills Springs in Kentucky in the middle of January. Ulysses Grant had made a name for himself at Fort Donelson even though he had thrown his men in a callous fashion at its breastworks. It appeared that the man had little concern for useless carnage, and his victory, I credit to incompetence on the Confederate side. The Battle of Mills Springs had more ominous implications. Unfortunately, General Thomas had performed brilliantly and had not lost anything from his military genius that I had witnessed in the Mexican War. Out of all the Northern generals, it was he whom I feared the most. My only hope was that he, being a Virginian, would never have Lincoln's trust. If he ever gained that trust, then he would be a general who could make the South lose the war.

I had heard so many stories about Lincoln and how clever he was. I didn't trust those stories. I believed he would never trust General Thomas, even though Thomas would be his most efficient general. Furthermore, in the statements he had made, especially the inaugural address, he had given off an aura of profound naïveté. It was like he never saw that the war was coming, and it was something that never could happen. It all seemed a shock to him. And then he had precipitated the crisis at Fort Sumter even though he didn't seem to know what would come next or how to fight this war that he'd had a hand in bringing about. His first round of soldiers had ninety-day enlistments. It would take ninety days just to get them trained and equipped to fight before their enlistments expired. Most would never see a single battle. The South needed to exploit Lincoln's naïveté to its advantage.

The press coverage of the Pea Ridge victory, much to my delight, hardly made a mention of the radical new tactic that I had used, smoke ordnance, or the critical part it had played in the victory. Rather, the coverage focused on the so-called atrocities that Pike's three regiments of Indians had committed against the Northern soldiers. The real story was the new tactic, but it seemed the atrocity allegations were all the Northern press was concerned about. And that was okay with me. Let them lose one or two more major battles due to my new tactics, and then maybe they would start to discover them. The real story that they missed was that the modern era had produced many new advancements that would change the conduct of warfare forever and that those who had the imagination to use them would be the great winners of history.

A week of rest and refit went by, and the time came to plan another move. I spent a few days in my tent because my blood was still too thin for the cold that I experienced out here. I had become so used to desert living that the temperatures of the North, even here in Arkansas, made me extremely uncomfortable. I had to wear two uniforms, one over the other, to try to maintain my body's warmth. In the desert we had to march in temperatures of one hundred–plus degrees for months at a time. We would move out by night and bivouac during the day sometimes when it got critically hot; nevertheless, there was no sleep to be had due to the heat. By contrast, here you had to keep marching or otherwise moving to stay warm. I so looked forward to the summer months.

I had contacted several of the officers I knew via mail or wire concerning concentrating forces for a move into the North sooner rather than later. General Jackson and I were on the same level as far as understanding the necessity to invade the North immediately. If I had more than my current force, then I could achieve it on my own. But if we went now, what I had would be little more than a large raiding party. I would need a force at least three times my current size in order to launch a war-winning invasion of the North. Where would I get such a force, and would God grant me one? That was my constant prayer. A western pincer to invade and envelop along with an eastern pincer: that was the way we had to win this war. So I must stay here on the defensive in the South and wait for my opportunity to gather this larger force. How I hated defensive battle.

Chapter 3

Shiloh

It was at this time, when I was pondering and praying after the victory of Pea Ridge, that I heard through the wires that something big was brewing in Tennessee. General Albert Sidney Johnston and General Beauregard were cooking something up to put an end to enemy triumphs in the west. Grant was riding high off of the victories at Forts Henry and Donelson. The more I learned about them, the more I thought the victories didn't have so much to do with the generals. The Confederate commander there had tried to launch an assault against the enemy that had no chance of success. This had only weakened the effective manpower. Grant had flung his command with little consideration for their lives. One of Grant's subordinates had come up with the tactics that led to the forts' surrender. The Northern papers, with their penchant for hyperbole, had made Grant a national hero overnight, calling him "Unconditional Surrender Grant," a play on his first two initials, US. Grant had served in Mexico honorably, but I had never known him other than as another face in the formations.

I thought Sherman was going to take command in the west because he came from a very connected political family. But he evidently had a nervous breakdown, and the high command relieved him. He had little combat experience and was more or less an army administrator. I heard thirdhand that he was very clever but too high-strung. With Sherman out of the way and Grant riding high, Washington would give Grant command in the west. Right now that army was getting ready to come down the Mississippi to try to cut the South into two pieces.

My victory at Pea Ridge had not changed the geometry of the Northern strategy. The strategists back in Washington would deal with the Trans-Mississippi at another time. The defeat was a minor setback not even worth noticing, and that suited me fine. They were minus a mere 10,000 soldiers that we had eliminated from the chessboard. It turned out to be more significant than that, but Washington treated the defeat as just a morale booster for the soon-to-be down-and-out Southerners, just like the fall of Fort Donelson had been a great morale booster for the North. As for me, the Northern papers, along with excoriating my Indian soldiers for their alleged atrocities, condemned me for being an uncivilized traitor and a disgrace to my father's memory. I was unconventional—that bit was true—but I was no more uncivilized than any other modern general. Pike's Indians provided me a distraction. It was better that the world focus on them and not on the other tricks that I had stowed in my supply trains. I didn't want the enemy to know about them until I had gotten a chance to employ them on the battlefield.

On the twelfth of March, I was able to establish communications with Old Bory's headquarters. The wire I received read, "Please take your army to the east with all possible speed to my area of operations. P. T. Beauregard." I issued orders on the thirteenth for my army to march on sunrise of the fifteenth. We had an inspection on the fourteenth. To a man, they were completely reshod, deloused, reclothed, and ready for action. Nearly half of the men had given up their rope belts and now wore the confiscated US belts upside down to show the SN.

"We are a new nation, the Southern Nation!" I hollered out to them. We would take the ideals of our fathers to new heights until we achieved freedom, peace, and plenty for all of our countrymen.

Once the news of our victory spread to northern Arkansas and Missouri, we were inundated with farmers driving herds of hogs at us. None of us had seen so much pork and bacon in one place in all of our lives. One farmer came into my camp and said, "General, my smokehouse is yours. Take all that you want and all that you need." The men had all that they could eat or carry. There were hundreds of skillets over campfires on those nights, with the boys frying pork and bacon until they could eat no more. But there was no waste. The men even ate the bacon drippings, mixing them with cornmeal or flour roasted over a fire. This was Southern hospitality at its best, I thought.

We still had paroled Northern soldiers with us after a week's time. I had told their General Curtis that I would detach a few companies of scouts to guide them out of Arkansas as far as the Kansas border. I forbade them to cross back over into Missouri or the Trans-Mississippi area of operations. We kept all of the division's muster rolls and told them that for the duration of the war, any men who ventured back into the area would be summarily shot as spies. Some of Curtis's men had refused to exchange their warm wool garments for Confederate rags and went back with clothing fashioned out of blankets. I did provide wagons for the transport of their wounded.

On the evening of the fourteenth, I sought out General Pike and spent the evening with him and his Indians. I sought out their medicine men, and we smoked the sacred pipe. Earlier that day Bory's headquarters had sent me information on Grant's order of battle, and I noticed that Sherman was out of the sanitarium and Grant had given him a division to command. One of the Cherokee medicine men spoke up and said to me that a message I had already received from an Indian spirit was now in effect. Immediately, I thought of Gopan's prophecy. He had told me that I would meet up with a badger and a fox and that I was to take them prisoner and never let them be free. After I considered who among the enemy had badger and fox tendencies, given current events, I decided it would have to be Grant and Sherman.

Grant was like a badger. He was blind to business and was a failure in business. But in warfare he was aggressive and no doubt would hold his own. Sherman was like a fox. He never stood still but spent the day scheming and making crafty plans. He was even redheaded like the red fox. After

I said good night to the medicine men, I knew in my soul that somehow I must capture this badger and fox. This was my mission now from the spirit world.

On the fifteenth of March, we set out on a journey across the length of northern Arkansas into Tennessee. I instructed a leisurely pace despite orders for all speed. I wanted the men to maintain the high levels of rest, hygiene, and energy that they had achieved. Haste makes waste, as the proverb goes. I wanted the men to keep their strength for as long as possible, at least until they got to where they were going. That way I could expect tigers on the battlefield that I would unleash on an exhausted, bedraggled enemy. We also would have no problems with stragglers. All men would be able to keep pace so that the 17,000-man force that I had started with would be a 17,000-man force when they got to the battle area. I ordered a pace of only twenty miles per day, with a full stand-down and bivouac day at the end of five days to clean, wash, and eat and maybe throw in a card game or two.

Also, it was critical for Price's and McCulloch's men to get to know each other better and set aside their differences. They might have started out as bitter enemies, but the time would come when they would need to fight as one army, and then they would become best friends. I knew Old Bory had ordered us to move with all speed, but I needed as much time as I could borrow to get the men healthy and welded together into one hard-hitting fighting force. And I didn't know what might lie ahead once we crossed the Mississippi into Tennessee. In Arkansas the food and hospitality of the people were first-rate, making my men stronger and their morale higher with each day that they spent in that state. They held their heads high through every town, where they bathed in the light of the adoration of the townsfolk. The people of the towns made no secret of their love of our army and cried tears of joy by the bucketful all along the way. There were salutes from little children, roads strewn with flowers, and hugs and kisses from the ladies. There was drink and food handed off to the men on the march. The men beamed with pride, and some even shed tears of joy of their own. I wanted this experience for them and to make it last as long as I could arrange it. I knew that they were heading for a desperate battle in a few days that would most likely determine whether the Southern Nation would become a reality or forever be a lost dream.

I was under no illusions. This next clash would shock the world in its carnage. We were shortly to see wholesale butchery of men in the tens of thousands in a single day. The world was oblivious to the fact that this was what modern warfare had come to. But in a few days, this was what was going to happen, and there was no stopping it.

Our army was up to strength, with all men accounted for. After the losses at Pea Ridge, we were at 17,000 effective. We were one full week into the march, including the full bivouac day that I had ordered. I then turned the army south toward Memphis. It was there that we would make our river crossing and hitch a ride on the railroad, heading east to hook up with Albert Sidney Johnston's main body in Tennessee.

On March 24, my staff and I started to get more detailed information on the enemy's movements. Grant had been moving his large force down the Tennessee River, accompanied by naval gunboats and transports. General Buell was behind him and expected to link up for a drive south, possibly toward the Mississippi. Generals Johnston and Beauregard were getting a large army together to meet them. I sent couriers out to get more precise word as to the timing and location of where this engagement might be. At some point, our leisurely pace might have to change to a double-quick, but I was still not yet alarmed. My men were having a great march, morale was sky-high, and I didn't want to put that to a premature end.

By the twenty-eighth of March, we had completed the turn south and were bearing down on Memphis. My advanced party of scouts had already made contact with the local authorities, giving them a chance to get things ready to receive our corps, 16,500 men with over 120 cannons. We were now cannon-heavy, having seized more than fifty cannons of the enemy. We also had a train of secret ordnance and the regular supply trains, which was large for a force of our size. We arrived at Memphis on the fourth of April. The authorities had stacked railroad cars once they learned of my plans to use the railroad. We would be little burden to their resources if they could move us along quickly, and rail would be the fastest way to get us out of the area.

Word at Memphis from army authorities was that Johnston and Beauregard had taken the whole army up from Corinth to attack Grant at Pittsburgh Landing. Now it was time for the double-quick. After a hurried loading onto railcars and a night and a day traveling via rail, we disembarked in the area of operations on the evening of the fifth. We reassembled and made plans for an all-night march into the morning of the sixth. I had no time to seek orders from higher headquarters. After studying a few of the local maps, we would be marching east-southeast and would hit Grant from the north down, from the direction of Crump's Landing. Fortunately, we had found a good road that paralleled the area. We stayed to the west of Johnston's army and then to the west of the enemy. My aim was to get our whole force to the north of the battlefield and then swing down and to the east in a battle line, making our presence felt in a 120-gun cannonade.

At dawn on the sixth, we could hear the opening of the battle to our east. We were still not north enough yet. At 10:00 a.m. I ordered the turn toward the east until we made contact with the Tennessee River. A scout reported it in sight around eleven o'clock. We were now in the enemy's rear. I ordered a movement to contact once our battle line formed. McCulloch's division was on the right; Price's was on the left. When we made contact, we found mobs of what appeared to be enemy stragglers who had abandoned their weapons. I decided to let them pass through our lines unmolested and get to our rear since they would only get in the way of our assault. Then we found more straggler groups and more and more. I hadn't fully comprehended what was happening. My staff grabbed a couple of men on the march and got as much information as possible given the circumstances. These beaten men were the remnants of formations that had absorbed Johnston's initial assault; they had not been dug in and had been completely unprepared for the enormity of the attack. How many waves of these men would we have to go through to get to the main body of resisting men?

When our line stretched across Snake's Creek, we could see heavy concentrations of blue off in the distance. I ordered all of my cannons forward immediately along the creek, and at two o'clock in the afternoon, on the part of the creek closest to the Tennessee River, we had eighty cannons lined up hub to hub. I gave the order to commence firing. A devastating blanket of cannon fire poured out over the enemy rear. What an opportunity for artillery! We were right in the middle of a dense concentration of enemy out in the open and unprotected, and there was nothing they could do about it. All of their cannons were deployed to the front, so there was no counter-battery fire for our gunners to contend with. For a full thirty minutes we kept up a hot fire that made the enemy formations dance away from the bouncing cannonballs, from their left, their right, and all directions. Then two black gunboats approached us from the river. I ordered the forty cannons we had on the river to engage. It was a mismatch. We fired incendiary shot, and fires broke out on the boats. They had to retreat back down the river to put out their fires. In the interim, our cannonade continued unchallenged.

At 4:00 p.m., the action ended with white flags. Firing stopped, and one after another, I accepted the surrenders of Hurlbert, Nelson, McClernland, and Sherman. I assumed that Grant would surrender formally to Johnston. I quickly sent detachments of men over the Snake Creek Bridge for the purpose of gathering all the weapons. The first order that I gave to the surrendering parties was to drop their weapons onto the ground. *How long is it going to take to gather up fifty thousand rifles?* I wondered. But I wanted them gathered up as quickly as possible. The sun would be down in a few hours, and I wanted these men out of the fight because Buell was coming up right behind us. My men finally ordered all the enemy to dump the weapons into great heaps, and we posted a heavy guard over them in preparation for the night. All things considered, the effort had taken less time than I had expected due to the energy and speed my men applied to the task.

I had yet to have any contact with my own high command. No doubt they were aware of our presence, had heard the deafening cannonade, and knew that we weren't just avenging angels from the Almighty but were a regular Southern army coming to their assistance. My last proper contact with high command had been weeks ago when I received the message from Old Bory to march east. Right now I was ensconced by a wall of surrendered enemy. I got a hold of some scouts attached to my staff and told them, "Get out there on the other side of the battlefield and see if you can find a general officer so I can get some orders."

Around 5:00 p.m. they came back, and the sergeant in charge said, "The lines are all mixed up. All the divisions are blended together, both friend and enemy. Our cannon fire is what caused the surrender. No one knows who we are or how we got here. Grant thinks you got forty thousand men behind you, sir."

"Did you find anyone in authority?"

"Yes, sir, we did. We found General Bragg's headquarters. His staff told us that General Johnston is dead, shot down around noon. General Beauregard's headquarters is down at a place called Shiloh Chapel. General Bragg's staff said they thought it might be us shooting up the enemy from behind, but they had no confirmation who it was."

"Has General Grant been taken prisoner yet?"

"No, not yet, and with all the chaos it might not be until tomorrow from what we heard."

"Well, boys, I'm taking it upon myself to find out where Grant is."

I ordered all available scouts to fan out and locate Grant. At 6:00 p.m. a scout private came up to me and said, "Sir, Grant is at Sherman's headquarters."

I said, "Order all the scouts to meet me there and to bring General Sherman with them." At 6:15 p.m. we arrived. I couldn't believe what a small battlefield this actually was to have so many men engaged in each other's destruction. I saw Grant and Sherman standing together outside of a tent. "General Grant, General Sherman, I am Major General Thomas Jenkins Worth, and you are my prisoners."

"I know who you are," Grant said. "You look exactly like your dad. Tell me, General, what's a Northern boy like you doing down here dressed up in a rebel officer uniform?"

"I would appreciate it, General, if you would not address me as a rebel officer. Loyalty to the written Constitution does not make one a rebel."

"Oh, I see, General. So you are one of the good guys?" he said in a contemptuous tone. "So now what are your plans for us?"

"General Grant, have no fear. I will not be giving you a parole, or General Sherman, but we will take good care of you. I have it all arranged. For you, this war is over. You are going to be taken by rail tomorrow morning to Memphis. From there you will go to a fort in Texas, very far from here, where although under constant guard, you will find plenty of the finest whiskey from Old Mexico and plenty of the best cigars in the territory for General Sherman. Please enjoy your forced retirement, compliments of the Southern army."

The men looked at each other, somewhat surprised. "Why won't you parole us?" Grant asked.

"Because, gentlemen, in order to parole you, we would have to exchange you for Southern generals of equal rank and importance to the war, and that isn't going to happen."

"One more thing, General Worth," said Grant. "You don't have to worry about gathering the weapons together in such a hurry. I gave orders for all resistance to end, and you should have no trouble."

With that we marched off back to my lines over the Snake Creek Bridge. It seems that all was chaos on the southern side of that bridge. Our army, that of the Trans-Mississippi, was the only army on the field unscathed and completely in order. As I put the two generals under a heavy guard, one of my scouts rode up in a lather. "General Worth, sir, large navy boats are heading down the river this way!"

"Send word over to my artillery commander—turn all cannons toward the river now! Got that, soldier?"

"Yes, sir, I got it!" The scout turned his mount around and headed toward the commander's tent.

"Oh my God, it's the transports," Grant said under his breath.

When I arrived at the riverbank, sure enough, a large,

poorly lit boat was steaming cautiously toward Pittsburgh Landing, followed by more dark hulks in the distance. I ordered a single cannon shot across the bow. A volley of musketry was the reply. Obviously, these were Buell's transports on which stood Buell's army—another unique opportunity for artillery. At that moment I had a single flare fired, which was our nighttime order to commence firing. The transport received a return volley of over one hundred solid cannon shots, to be quickly reloaded with incendiary. The half of the transport that faced west, the cannonade reduced to splinters. Then the guns fired at will up and down the line. Within minutes the leading ship started to show a list. Fires broke out all over the vessel. Men abandoned the hulk on its eastern side before it became totally engulfed in flames, after which I ordered a cease-fire. The survivors swam to the opposite shore, where they either would escape into the night or would be picked up by Southern patrols. The other boats in the line quickly either reversed course to go back up the river or beached on the far side of the river as they were about to come within range of our cannons. Our pickets fished a few of the men out of the water and gained confirmation that indeed this was Buell's army. If another day had passed, our army's victory would have turned out quite differently.

At about 9:00 p.m., a runner came up from Beauregard's headquarters with a request that I come see him. At last, I would get to reconnect with high command. When I got to his headquarters, Beauregard saluted me first, which I thought a bit unusual. I returned the salute. Then he came up and grabbed me in an uncharacteristic bear hug. "Thank

God you came! You saved us! I just heard about Buell's transports. You have smashed our enemies, saved this army, and saved the South! God bless you, my boy! Indeed, you are just as gifted and talented as your father. I knew it after your victory at Pea Ridge. Here is the son of the hero of Mexico come to save the South! And by God, you have done so. You have come like a thunderbolt out of the sky to scatter our enemies. Your father was the greatest soldier I ever knew, and you are the same as he. You have caused the surrender of two Northern armies in a month's time. Who would have thought it possible? You will certainly be given command of this army, and I will be the first to recommend it."

"What makes you say that, sir?" I questioned.

"Because Jeff Davis and I don't get along very well, and he admired your father. You have proven beyond any doubt that you are just as brilliant as he. You will get command of all the western armies very shortly. I, for one, will make that abundantly clear to them. Who would have thought that a bunch of frontiersmen from beyond the great river would smash the army of Grant? That could have happened only under brilliant leadership. It could have happened only at the hands of the son of the magnificent General William Jenkins Worth!"

"Well, sir, I hope your faith in me is not premature. It is quite a step from corps to theater command."

"You will get it, and you will lead us to victory just like you have today," said a jubilant Old Bory.

"Can I ask the details of General Johnston's death?"

Beauregard's face suddenly changed from light to dark. "He was shot in the leg and bled to death."

"Shot in the leg?" I said.

"Yes," said Beauregard. "He had sent his surgeons off to help enemy prisoner wounded, so he bled to death."

Here it is again, I thought, *the misplaced Southern chivalry.* It could have cost us this battle and God knows whatever else after. If my corps had not arrived at the exact time and place that it did, the battle would have been lost and the war also. If we had failed to knock out Grant and his army in this battle, then we would have lost the war for the South, no question. And with Johnston dead on the field at the most critical point in the battle, there was no way the men could have encircled Grant on their own without the appropriate guidance and orders. Historians would later say that this date in history and this battle were the moment when we created the Southern Nation. But how many more times must I witness this defect of the Southern nobility? Obviously, a leg shot is not enough to kill a man if there are sufficient medical people in the area or even a backwoodsman who knows how to tie off a limb to stop the flow of blood. But Johnston had sent his medical people off to tend the enemy, despite what his loss might mean to the entire war effort. How insane, how irresponsible to die of a leg wound. And all because he had to be noble? Johnston had been a lion among men, and there were no limits to my admiration for him. His loss was a terrible tragedy for us. He was a commander we desperately needed to win this war.

"General Beauregard, I am your subordinate and await your orders."

"General Worth, right now you must see to your men's needs. How many causalities did you suffer?"

"Actually, sir, I don't think we took any—none that I saw. I can account for all the cannon crew, and the infantry never had to engage. They served as a demonstration. And one of my scouts reported that the enemy counted them twice as large as they actually were."

"Unbelievable, General—a truly incredible performance! Right now I do request that you send out your patrols to find out what became of Buell's army. If we catch up with them, they are the last great formation of the Northern army left in the west. Just think of that for a moment. We have a chance to liberate our nation in the west! It is the only thing that keeps my spirits up after the horrible losses of this day. Good night, General Worth, and a million thanks for your miraculous deeds of this day. All of the South will rejoice in this great victory that you have given us. Let the church bells ring!"

Chapter 4

Nashville

There is a saying among the soldiers that "the sun doesn't shine on the same dog's ass all the time." With the victory at Shiloh, I could feel the warmth of the sunlight starting to shine on me. Old Bory had pretty much stepped aside to let me take over command of the entire Army of the West in an informal capacity going forward. I gave orders to my Trans-Mississippi corps to show the great army of Johnston how we did things when absorbing the assets of a defeated army. First, all of our soldiers proceeded to get fed, shod, and clothed properly using the captured enemy supply trains. We issued rations to every man, all he could eat and carry. All of our men traded up on their weapons and discarded outdated ones. We would see no more of Grandpa's Kentucky long-bore, of which unbelievably we had seen more than a few. Everyone who wanted them now had factory-new, percussion-capped, rifled Springfields courtesy of our Northern cousins' arms factories. The men of Johnston's army also traded in their homespun rags for nicely fitted, machine-stitched wool uniforms, which the Northern factories made to military specifications and which we promptly dyed the color gray. Coffee was flowing freely again. The men took rancid biscuits full of worms and weevils out of their rucksacks and fed them to the horses, mules, and hogs. Our men got hardtack that was fresh and free of bugs. The rope belts also disappeared, and the SN of the upside-down US belts appeared.

The disposition of the enemy army became more of an issue. We couldn't parole them because there was no easy way to get them back to their own lines. Moreover, we couldn't turn them loose with any assurance that they wouldn't just get new arms and new supplies up north and be sent back at us to fight again. There were too many of them. I estimated some 50,000 men. For now we needed to keep them as prisoners of war whom we could release at a later time. I sent word to all local authorities to provide enough constabulary and militia to guard them in camps until we could sort out their fate later—not much later, we hoped, because 50,000 men were a lot of mouths to keep fed.

As far as the strategic consequence of our situation, the momentum had decisively swung our way. The victory at Shiloh was key to ultimate victory in the war. When we considered what a close shave the whole thing had turned out to be, we had infinite reasons to give thanks and much to celebrate. Without this victory, our path to ultimate victory would have been close to impossible. It was only a question of time before the North got its war machine into gear and turned from sleeping giant into juggernaut. The

North's loss at Shiloh would prove to be the sawing off of a leg of a four-legged chair, with the remainder teetering in the balance. And the destruction of Buell's force would provide that push we needed in our direction. We would immediately be able to invade Ohio and sack cities such as Cincinnati, unmolested by any organized formation of regulars. Washington would have to either split its army in the east to attack us or let us split the Union in two, getting stronger, not weaker, as we made our way for the final assault on the North. We made up in fighting spirit and finesse what we lacked in matériel. But we would get that too in our invasion. We would sack or destroy everything of military value and ship south everything we could not carry. In the North General McClellan had taken over the army from the old fop Scott, and word was that he had organized a very formidable force on the Potomac with endless supplies of manpower and matériel. They were all massing and drilling for a grand invasion of the South. To what extent their plans would change if we were to invade the North first, we would have to find out. But in order to do that, we would have to deal with Buell. Our army would have no resources to draw from once we got north of the Mason–Dixon line. We would have to live off of enemy resources 100 percent. The only thing we would get from the South would be more men, more divisions as they became available.

I went over these plans almost nightly with Beauregard. And we were thinking along the same lines as Johnston had and as Jackson did. We had no choice but to take the fight to the enemy and not wait for the enemy to come down

South again. It was only some Southern gentlemen who hung around the offices at Richmond who didn't seem to have a full grasp of the peril the nation was in. But the issue was deeper than that. The Southern gentlemen wanted to fight the war based on the laws of misguided chivalry. This was a bugaboo that hung over us like a dark cloud. But it was something of our own making, deep within the minds and hearts of our political leaders, and was almost a greater threat to us than the guns of the enemy. These leaders had serious misgivings about conducting warfare on a civilian population, although I was convinced that the leaders of the North, such as Grant and Sherman, had no such misgivings about making war on the Southern population. And it would be a matter of natural logic to them to raise up more such leaders.

I was taken aback by Grant's callous attitude toward his own men, having not even given his men the order to entrench at Shiloh. This was a continuation of his callousness at Donelson. If he fought with such little regard for his own men, then he would have no qualms about waging total war against innocent civilians. There was no misguided chivalry in his attitude. He was not encumbered. He fought like a man with unlimited resources, and in reality, he had no problem with resources like we had. To him it was a mathematical process. All he needed was a draw to achieve victory because there were always more men and matériel to draw from at his back. As long as he could keep fighting in the field by day and killing his conscience at night with whiskey, then ultimate victory for him was only a matter of time. Johnston had attacked Grant's men on an open battlefield with no works to protect them. But Grant had known that Buell was right behind him and that sheer weight of numbers would eventually carry the day. Sherman wouldn't send out patrols despite evidence that some of his men knew that the Southern army was right outside his perimeter, ready to pounce upon him. If men of this attitude cared so little for the lives of their own men, then what would they do to us if we were ever at their mercy? But making Jeff Davis and the perfumed politicians in Richmond understand this would be a formidable battle in itself. This is not to say that I did not respect Jeff Davis. I loved the man and was grateful that he had become our leader. But those wonderful and noble ideas of his might get us all killed.

The one secret weapon that I had, despite being born and raised in the North, was the high esteem that the Southern gentlemen seemed to have for the memory of my father. It was as if my father were still alive and fighting for the South in my body. I heard this over and over again. Anyone who had known my father or had fought under him, which was virtually the entire West Point officer corps that had fought in Mexico, remarked about my looks and mannerisms and would comment on how he saw my father in me. This included Old Bory and Jeff Davis himself, who had worked with him in Mexico personally. When they saw me, they expected to see nothing less than the brilliance and efficiency that my father had demonstrated throughout his career. And so far I had not disappointed them. I could see it in Old Bory's eyes when he looked at me. It was like he was looking at an angel sent from the Almighty who would lead the South to victory. He was most gracious to me always and made no secret of the fact that he was going to lobby Davis to relinquish command of the entire Army of the West over to me. I was always too busy to be embarrassed by all this. And the adulation of the newspapers toward me was excessive in my opinion. The *Charlotte Observer* called me "General Thomas Jenkins Worth, the Alexander the Great of the Southern cause," and compared Shiloh to the Battle of Issus. I held my opinions to myself, however, as I could see that the myth growing about me would be a great tool in the psychological battle we were also waging against our enemy. Such prestige, such honor, would give our army a huge psychological and morale-building edge against those who would face us in the immediate future. And the ultimate victory of our army was all that I cared about.

To that battle immediately ahead, General Forrest had sent out cavalry patrols all the way to Nashville to cover every possible avenue where the enemy might move. After three days it became clear that Buell was falling back with his entire army to hide behind the defenses at Nashville. All of us had predicted that this was his most logical move. He was really in a bad position. If he were to give up Nashville, then the North would not be able to mount another threat to the west for a considerable time. From Nashville, he would get constant support via rail from the North and might be able to hold out for another army that the North could marshal together, allowing the Union to maintain its presence in the theater. They would prepare for a siege, no doubt, but I was not going to allow them the opportunity to have that. We had no time for a siege. Time for the South, even in the light of the victory at Shiloh, was running out. We had no choice but to do our reconnaissance, conduct our attack, overrun the enemy, and then move on to the next target. We had to advance from one victory to the next in rapid succession if we were to have a chance at overall victory. Pea Ridge had begun this process. Shiloh had continued it, and Nashville would be next.

The fourth day after the victory at Shiloh had passed. Buell's army had arrived at the defensive works at Nashville and would be shortly digging in and improving them. In the meantime, our army had enjoyed ample rest, resupply, reorganization, and refitting. Old Bory had now issued orders that I had prepared for the operation. We moved out 60,000 effectives fully equipped with over three hundred cannons, that which we had brought and many that we had seized. We had a huge supply train, having taken the best of all the equipment plus enemy field kitchens. The idea was to have a well-rested, well-fed army that would have the strength to launch an overpowering lightning attack on Nashville. There would be no prolonged siege. We didn't want the enemy to be able to summon up any significant reinforcements from the North. Elimination of that army off of the chessboard was the only guarantee of that. We were to absorb this army just as we had absorbed the others over the past month. The springtime weather was becoming warmer and drier. I was finally able to take off that second uniform that I wore under my normal uniform to stay warm. This would make me more nimble just in case I had to use my saber. The men were in high morale and were fit and trim. I was amused by the attitude of the soldiers spurring on their generals in this time of high expectations. "Let's get this war over with, General, so I can get back to the wife and the young'uns." This was what I would hear on the march. I was sure it was our militiamen saying that. How many militiamen in history, I wondered, could boast of participating in one of the most crucial victories ever?

On we marched northward. The people of Franklin gave a rousing display of thanks to our army. We came from eight out of the eleven Southern states. We were a triumphant Southern army that had slung the rock at Goliath's forehead and had now taken up the sword that would sever that head. We made the march to Nashville in three days with hardly a skirmish. The enemy had gotten word to all its forces in the area to come back to Nashville and prepare for the siege in hope of reinforcements to come from the east. The word I was getting from intelligence sources was that no such reinforcements adequate to relieve a siege were coming anytime soon. The priority for Washington was the mounting of the long-awaited drive to Richmond. A huge army of over 100,000 under General McClellan was waiting for orders to invade. Lincoln was not going to let anything interfere with that invasion. But it was a mistake to leave Buell by himself. Although it was true that all this fighting was happening on Southern soil, once we had destroyed Buell's army, nothing could stop us from going on into Ohio. Then we would make Lincoln shed bitter tears. He couldn't see that now, but soon it would become his reality. Ohio was at the very heart of the North, with great industrial cities in close proximity. Once we had feasted off of the abundance in these cities, we would make our grand march to the east and link up with our eastern armies for the coup de grâce.

Nashville was a city established in a great pocket that the Cumberland River had formed over the millennia. The enemy had seized it in February and had constructed a line of hasty entrenchments and fortified works. They had not had enough time to improve these to the extent necessary to withstand an army of 60,000 exploding on the city from the South. Nevertheless, I was not going to fling the army at this line willy-nilly. I didn't believe in throwing men's lives away in a suicidal frontal assault—not with today's .50-caliber rifle. No one wants to die at an early age, and if you can just convince the enemy that he will die if he doesn't surrender first, then you have saved yourself and him.

From all accounts, we were facing the Army of the Ohio, with some 20,000 effectives. No substantial formations had escaped the Shiloh pocket from Grant's Army of the Tennessee, just a few swimmers who had made it to the other side of the river hatless and weaponless. The once-great Army of the Tennessee was no longer our concern but was the responsibility of the constabulary and local militia where we had left them.

The deployments around Nashville went thus: Out of the five corps total, to my left were two corps from the Army of Mississippi that Generals Polk and Breckenridge commanded. On my right were another two corps under the commands of Bragg and Hardee. In the center was my own corps of the Trans-Mississippians. This would be a different kind of assault. We would not be demonstrating or feinting to try and draw away enemy units. We wanted to hit the enemy strongpoint, which went against military logic of the day. There would be no flanking maneuvers, no grand right wheels, and no grand left wheels requiring complex ordering and marching with all the accompanying miscommunications, unanticipated obstacles, and confusions. This was because of the new weapon I would unveil on the battlefield for the first time. I wasn't sure myself how to classify this weapon. Was it a weapon of artillery or one of infantry? Since I would be using artillery crews to serve it, I would have to classify both the weapon and the assault as an artillery operation.

Ensconced in the supply train that I had brought to Arkansas all the way from the gunsmith shops of the old Department of Texas were the guns based on Gatling's designs. I had used every penny of my inheritance from my father to build eight of these guns along with their carriages and special ammunition. We now deployed them with their specially trained crews along the concave line that extended around the Nashville entrenchments in the area of the Harding Pike leading into Nashville. The tactic we would employ was simple. The eight guns would be divided into four fire teams. The teams would move out in front of the infantry. One team would bound for about one hundred yards while the other would provide covering fire for the movement. Then they would switch off. The bound would switch to fifty yards, then twenty-five, until all eight guns would deploy together on one line. The result would be the enemy line coming under constant, withering fire sweeping back and forth. This continuous strafing of the enemy line would not allow the individual enemy soldiers to lift their heads long enough above their entrenchments to get off an aimed shot, let alone a coordinated volley with their comrades. All of the time that this was going on, we would have two hundred cannons concentrated hub to hub behind our bounding guns that would first and foremost provide counter-battery fire to the enemy's dug-in cannon and second reduce strong battlements and poke holes through the enemy line in preparation for the infantry assault. Also, on each end of the Cumberland River, we would have strong reinforced batteries of our remaining cannons to ward off any enemy gunboats that might attempt support and to seal off yet another river pocket to trap Buell and his army from the possibility of escape. The objective of both the special artillery and the conventional artillery would be to reduce the entrenchments and completely denude them of enemy riflemen on the Harding Pike, so that I could pour infantry regiments through the breech. The men could at that point, at the discretion of their commanders, reduce the enemy line from behind up and down that line. Once we initiated and exploited the breakthrough, we could immediately redeploy the special artillery up onto high points forward, where they could sweep concentrations of enemy at will with rapid fire. My prediction was that the enemy would quickly fold under the shock of the new weaponry in tandem with the concentrated cannonade.

It was the morning of April 16. Word came back that Forrest's cavalry had cut the rail line from the north into Nashville. He had also cut all telegraph communications into the city. Buell could no longer communicate with Washington. Forrest had conducted extensive reconnaissance patrols the week prior and eventually had sent his entire division across the Cumberland River in anticipation of the encirclement. Buell had no escape route out of Nashville at this point. A normal siege would take weeks and might even have provoked a relief army from Washington to contest it. What Buell didn't know was that there would be no siege. He was about to become the victim of modern warfare with its modern weaponry and lightning tactics. No one would be there to save him or his army. Forrest had closed the back door.

At dawn, I sent word for the artillery on Montgomery Hill to commence firing. After a half-hour bombardment, all of the enemy cannon positions were engaged in counter-battery fire. Our batteries began to silence them one by one. Forty-five minutes into this process, I deemed it safe to advance the special artillery. The fire teams went forward in an uninterrupted leapfrog relay advance toward the enemy line. Eventually, all eight guns made it on line and kept up a heat like no one before had ever seen. It was the equivalent of a whole infantry division's rate of fire all on one small point on the line nonstop. Our conventional artillery at the same time kept up a terrific rate of cannon fire from two hundred guns, blasting hole after hole in the enemy's works. In less than two hours nothing but splinters and ashes was left of an eighth-of-a-mile stretch of the enemy's line that had previously blocked the Harding Pike. I ordered the Trans-Mississippian corps forward. We had broken the spine of the entrenched line. Most of the enemy had retreated behind an inner line of entrenchments. There would be no envelopment of the enemy at the outer line of defensive works now that they had abandoned it wholesale. Once this became evident, I ordered my entire line forward.

By noontime the cannon that we had previously posted on Montgomery Hill had limbered up and unlimbered forward, occupying Lawrence Hill. At one o'clock I gave the order to commence fire on the enemy's inner works. Counter-battery fire took place for the next hour. A two o'clock, the artillery preparation and reduction of the enemy's works was sufficient to bring forward the special artillery up the Harding Pike once again. The strategy had similar results. The effect of the special artillery once again froze the enemy riflemen and snipers in place. They were unable or unwilling to stick their heads up above cover to take an accurate shot. Those who did fell with horrific head wounds and died from shots to the head with a grizzly rapidity. The scene became a grotesque display of headless bodies piling up behind the enemy trenches. Once again, it became evident to us that a breech had developed along the Harding Pike. Scouts and pickets that we sent forward found a no-man's-land of lifeless bodies and a crumbled resistance. I ordered another infantry assault. They charged forward at the double-quick and this time found the enemy rear to be in the streets of Nashville itself.

The inner line of entrenchments had collapsed as quickly and completely as the outer line had. I gave the order for a general advance by all divisions. The main body of the enemy force, now little more than a panicked mob of blue uniforms, made for the center of Nashville.

At four o'clock a white flag of truce came out of the city and toward our lines. After receiving reports that Forrest had shut down the line of retreat across the Cumberland and the telegraph communications, Buell had evidently decided that he had had enough. He was caught in the trap, and there was no way out.

I had first met with Forrest, a colonel at the time, at Shiloh, immediately after the battle. I'd gotten a chance to ask him about Grant and the events at Donelson. He confirmed for me that the fort did not have to fall. The issue had been confused leadership among our commanders and reports of enemy reinforcements that turned out to be fake. Forrest had ordered his regiment of cavalry to escape in a fit of disgust and protest. Forrest was a true believer in the cause of the Southern Nation and was not one afraid to carry the load himself and make the thing happen. He was a natural-born leader who had joined the army as a private and who paid to equip his regiment out of his own pocket. He was a stern, imposing figure with powerful convictions. Though I greatly respected his exuberance, I had wondered about those convictions and where they had led. He had been not just a slave owner but a slave trader before the war and had enough wealth to outfit Southern regiments. But yet he'd had the humility to join and train as a private and had not assumed that he should be given a colonelcy or generalship based on his wealth or status in society. I didn't know what he intended for himself after this war, but I certainly needed his so-far brilliant service and was grateful for it. He was smart, tough, and full of tenacity. These were qualities that the Southern army needed in all its men if it was to achieve victory.

The work of this day had gone as violently and as

quickly as a thunderbolt in a rainstorm and mercifully so. The special artillery and the accommodation of our armed formations to the new tactics were the reason for this. The special crews had performed splendidly. The enemy soldiers sitting behind their parapets and trenches had gotten chewed up unmercifully if they tried to fight, and our solid-shot cannonade had pounded them into the dust if they tried to stay put and sit it out along the areas where we concentrated our fire up the Harding Pike. Once again, I had used Pike's three regiments of Indians as my shock troops in the vanguard of the infantry assault. They had performed their mission as they had at Pea Ridge, with the exception of any scalpings or desecrations this time. The rest of my corps had known what to do without my having to tell them in so many words. Punch the hole and pour through: it was that simple. This was the new way—no need for far-flung movements or long, intricate commands.

At five in the afternoon on the sixteenth, the first and only day of this battle for Nashville, my scouts located and took into custody Generals Buell and Thomas and began escorting them to where I was posted at Lawrence Hill. There the generals would formally surrender their swords. General Beauregard had moved his headquarters twice during the day in a vain attempt to keep up with the rapidly moving events. He now was on his way up from Shy's Hill on horseback to Lawrence Hill. I assumed he would reach me at the same time as Generals Buell and Thomas.

All three generals came within sight at approximately five thirty in the afternoon. I received Old Bory first, and he gave me a somewhat uncharacteristic hug. "General Worth, what a magnificent job you have done today! Who would have thought we could take the city in a single day? You, sir, *are* the Alexander the Great of the South!"

"Well, General," I said, "I just used the common sense that God has given any soldier. The Almighty has given me enough sense to exploit the new tools that modern science provides that anyone could have used. It's up to all of us to either live in the future or die in the past."

"General," Old Bory continued, "I am not taking an ounce of credit for either this victory or Shiloh. I have just been an observer here who watched you conduct these marvels. I am formally requesting that Richmond award you overall command of this army. I will word it in such a way as to make it critical that they give you this command for the quickest and most efficient path to victory and an end to this catastrophic war. You alone have the grasp and have utilized the tactics that have resulted in a complete victory with minimal bloodshed for our side. Just think, General—you have eliminated three enemy armies from the field in six weeks. Right now we are unchallenged in this theater. The war, thanks to you, is already half-won!"

"General," I said, "I appreciate your vote of confidence, but I wish to remind you that if my army of Trans-Mississippians had arrived just one day later than they had at Shiloh, we would have had a very different outcome. Buell's army would have crossed onto Pittsburg Landing and saved Grant, and things would have developed much differently. And even now, unless we forge ahead with all speed, we might still lose this great advantage that we now have. I am certain that the wires from Washington will be burning with plans to force our decline from this lofty achievement. Our lucky victory at Shiloh will prove to be the key to ultimate victory, a key that we cannot lose. Let us pray that the good Southern gentlemen who are our masters in Richmond will give us a free hand to finish this thing. General, we have no time to waste in our planned invasion of the North. That has to come now. If this war goes on much longer, then we will fall into a war of attrition, which we cannot possibly win. Look at the men the North has picked for leaders, men such as Grant and Sherman, men who would think nothing of flinging thousands of their own into the furnace of certain death. When the North has summoned up enough men and matériel, they will use such men as this to heap wave after wave of fully equipped armies upon our land, and there will be no way for us to stop them."

"After what I have witnessed here today and over the last few weeks, General Worth, I am certain that you are the man who can stop them and lead us all the way to victory. I will make sure that Richmond knows that."

I turned my attention to Generals Buell and Thomas. General Buell made his way over to General Beauregard to offer his sword. Beauregard gestured to Thomas, to indicate he should offer his sword to me. I'd had vague contact with Buell during the Mexican War, but I'd had extensive contact with Thomas. I respected and admired him greatly, and it troubled me to see him in this situation. In my opinion, he had more raw talent and brains as a soldier than all the rest of the Northern general officer corps put together. And he was a Southerner from Virginia. Of all the enemy generals,

I had feared his prowess the most. He was as unwavering in battle as an iron leg trap was against a bear.

"General Worth, it is my duty to offer you my sword in surrender," Thomas said in a firm martial voice.

"You may keep your sword, General Thomas, although I do accept your surrender. It is a strange war, is it not? Here I am, a born and bred Northerner fighting for the South, and you a Southerner fighting for the North. But I dare say that my reception in the South has been much different than yours has been in the North. The Southern soldiers have placed in me an absolute trust, whereas I perceive that you, as a Virginian, people in high places have treated with skepticism. Otherwise, they wouldn't be putting inferior men over you."

"General Worth, it is not up to me to question the motives of my superiors. It is up to me to follow and obey orders according to the regulations."

"How has your family taken your defection to the other side?" I asked.

"My two sisters have disowned me," he said.

"Just like mine have disowned me," I responded. "What made you do it, George? What made you give up Virginia for the North?"

"I had to do it for my wife's sake," he answered. "My duty to my wife comes before the state of Virginia and it's political beliefs. Perhaps if it weren't so wedded to the idea of slavery, I might feel differently."

"I'm not a believer in slavery either, George. And the one thing I can promise you is that slavery is going to end one way or another. None of the most important Southern generals, when you talk to them in private, will tolerate this situation as it now stands once the war is over. They all resent the fact, as I do, of having to fight this horrendous war, which is a bloodbath, on our own soil because of the failure of the politicians to compromise in the courts and in the Congress and settle the issue of slavery peacefully. George, I still look up to you now as I did in Mexico. I sent Grant and Sherman off to an indefinite stay in Texas, under custody, for the duration of the war. I will not agree to have that done to you. We will parole you on condition that you never fight for the North again in this war. I will accept your word on that without further question. But I also want to offer you the opportunity to fight on our side, the side of your homeland, Virginia. I will make a recommendation that Richmond assign you a division immediately, should you be willing to accept."

"I am very sorry, General, that I can't take you up on your gracious offer. I must decline. It is not that I am ungrateful. It is because my own personal honor will not allow me to do that."

"Very well, George. Then this war is over for you. I do have your word that you will not again take up your sword against us?"

"I don't think President Lincoln will have much use for me after today. You have my word that I shall retire."

"Goodbye, George. Please enjoy the rest of your life as a civilian."

"I intend to, General, and I do pray that this war will come to a speedy end along with slavery."

Although the men were too tired to celebrate their

victory, the night of April 17 was a very hopeful one. The fighting would not resume at daybreak. Instead, a triumphant march through a liberated Southern city would ensue. And then, as my Army of the West and as the Army of Mississippi had done before, we would deliver a sober processing of the Army of the Ohio in which our men would get what they needed first out of the seized provisions, clothing, and equipment. We had all the arms and cannons that we could handle. The surplus, we would send south to arm new armies of recruits. The Army of the Ohio would then go the way of the Army of the Tennessee, off to camps that Southern constabulary and militia would run.

The morning of the eighteenth arrived. We had detachments of all the different divisions take their turn in parade-marching through the city of Nashville. They marched to wild and boisterous singing, bell ringing, and band playing in which their Southern patriotic songs could be heard nonstop. I decided not to enter the city but to stay at my Lawrence Hill headquarters, gathering data for the next operations plan for the next phase of the war: the invasion of the North. This would require a rapid march through Kentucky on our way to Ohio, with the first target being the city of Cincinnati.

The Battle of Nashville had ended the existence of regular Northern military formations in the west. The entire high command and regular officer corps, along with the cadre of noncommissioned officers and their legions of soldiers, we had taken off of the chessboard for good. We expected to face local Northern militia from here on out. They would not have the capability to organize or maneuver any large combat formations or have anyone in charge with the knowledge to do so. The soldiers in our army, on the other hand, were now all skilled veterans. And the recruiting efforts were very positive. Men from all over the South wanted to take part in this drubbing of the invaders. We started being very selective as to whom we would accept. Pike's three regiments of Indians, for example, accepted only other Indian recruits from the Indian Territories. And they did not take them all but rather turned some away. They were up to strength once again, as were all the divisions in our organization, despite taking heavy losses as the vanguard in the battles of the past month and a half. We even saw Missourians and Texans make the long trips and cross the Mississippi so that they could be with their friends already in the ranks. We witnessed many happy reunions of friends and family who had caught up with us and joined the ranks at Nashville.

At six in the evening, I decided to have a long and leisurely dinner with General Albert Pike, my subordinate.

"What are your plans now, General Worth?" he asked. "I know you will be anxious to get going in a few days."

"Yes, Al, I will be. But unfortunately, we used up eight of the ten wagonloads of special ammunition for our special artillery. We also haven't yet received a resupply of the smoke ordnance we used up at Pea Ridge. So all the special weapons capabilities that are directly responsible for two out of our three victories are out of the picture for now. I really don't want to invade the North without those capabilities back. But every day we hold back erodes the precious advantage for success that we now have. That opportunity won't be there very long. The news of our victory will put Lincoln under enormous pressure. The wave of alarm that it will cause will only make him redouble his efforts at our destruction. The bear is always most dangerous when you corner it. It's only a question of where he will lash out. Will it be in the east, or will he march his legions back out here to the west? The picture may change inside of a month.

"It might be good for us to stay here for a bit—build up our infrastructure and the railhead. We will be keeping the boys busy. I have engineer staff working on plans to build Nashville up into a larger military base than it already is. We have unlimited manpower with the army here, and we can put up scores of warehouses to store our arms and create space for gunsmiths and armorers. We can construct ordnance workshops for cannon-casting foundries and assembly shops for our new artillery. General Beauregard gave me a hint of what is going on back east. A large enemy force has been landing on the coast of Virginia on the peninsula. I would guess that they have been putting this plan together for a long time and that nothing, not even what we have done, is going to change that now. General Lee says that it will be the main invasion of the south that Washington has been building up to for the last six months. We also have information that the size of the invasion is enormous—some 200,000 effectives that their war department has fed, trained, and fully equipped. They appear now to be fully committed to this invasion despite events out here. Nevertheless, we will have to keep a sharp eye out for anything coming this way. My gut is telling me that they are obsessed with capturing Richmond. They have to ignore us for now. I don't expect them to halt their invasion. As long as we stay on Southern soil, then they will not go all out to fight us."

"But General Worth, you are an eastern boy yourself. May I speak candidly?"

"Of course, Al. Please unburden yourself."

"Well, sir, please don't take offense, but while the people of the South are rejoicing in our great victories, I am not sure they understand why you are out here doing what you are doing. Are you proslavery? What is a Southern gentleman to do if he doesn't have a barn full of slaves to order around? How does the honor culture of the Southern gentleman survive if you take away his slaves?"

"That's a very good question and one I need to answer for you, Al. First of all, I am not a Southern gentleman, it is true. Nor do I aspire to be one. I am an engineer who sees a giant boulder that needs to move from one point over to another in the quickest, most efficient way. My task is to see this done scientifically, not to try to conjure up a way to do it as King Arthur and his knights would. I see enormous defects in the Southern way of thinking as well as the North's. This war is an opportunity to fix them both. Sometimes ideas crop up in a society from necessity. Those ideas serve their purpose for a time and then need to be gone. Slavery is one such idea whose time has come and gone. Southern gentlemen are going to have to find a way to prove their honor other than owning slaves."

"But General, that is treason you are speaking."

"No, it's not treason; it's common sense. In my mind, it's treason to hold on to outdated ideas that threaten your survival as a nation. The North will never accept the existence of a slave state on the same continent as itself. Even if we are to win terms of peace and recognition, it will only be a respite. War will flare up again in another generation, and slavery will be its battle call. We are not strong enough to conquer the North. Even now, they are not fighting with both full fists. We haven't even sampled their full might. The only hope we have to create a permanent Southern Nation is to disgorge ourselves of the need for slavery. The truth is we don't need it at all. The South has unlimited resources and is waiting for the manpower to develop while the Northern cities are bulging with immigrants looking for work. Why not marry the two together? The South does not have to whip defenseless men to death in the fields to pick cotton. Such a thing is immoral and cannot continue. The North, on the other hand, has to learn about boundaries. The citizens of the South are a separate people with their own traditions and way of life. We can handle our own problems. The North added to those problems when they instituted the cotton tariff and decided to have it pay for all the expenses of their government. They need to find a legitimate way to finance their government, not hypocritically off the backs of slaves that they purport to want to free in their holier-than-thou pronouncements. They need to back off and let us fix the problem that they caused. Our victory in this war will solve both problems."

"Are you sure about that, General? Do you really think that the Southern gentlemen in Richmond are going to dispense with their lifestyles on the plantations once you get them this great victory?"

"It's really simple, Al—you replace one idea with another. Slavery and Christianity are completely contradictory ideas. How Christian is it to whip a man to death in a cotton field? Most of these slave folk themselves are Christians. This is an absurd inconsistency. It was the money men and the overseers, many from the North, who corrupted the original social structure so as to feed the cotton gins. This war is a punishment for that corruption, and the true-believing Christians are the ones who will see that. You find them in churches in every town and city in the South. They are your answer to the Southern gentlemen. The corruption of money based on slavery has made a mockery out of Southern society and any claims it has to the moral high ground. The Southern gentlemen do not walk in the footsteps of King Arthur and his knights, no matter how much they think they do. The noble nature of the Southern gentleman is preposterous in the reality of today's society. I myself am not a Christian, even though I was born and raised one. I consider myself a spiritualist. The hometown papers that I used to receive and the stories of the exploits of the Fox sisters were very intriguing. But I have found that all religions, be they Christian or spiritualist, believe in the basic equality of all people. We all have the divine spark within us regardless of our state in life or where we were born or what race we happened to be born into. You know yourself, Al, that I spend more of my free time, what little I have, talking to your Indians, whom I consider closer to me in belief than the white men."

"So you see no difference between the slaves and the whites? I still don't see how you are going to change things, but then I didn't see how you were going to crush three Northern armies either!"

"That's right, Al. I see no difference. We are all spiritual beings on a spiritual journey who have the divine spark within us. And the Southern Christians, once they take a step back after having washed away all this blood from the war, will see that too. If humans were not spiritual beings, then they would not be born to die. Sooner or later, we all have to come to grips with our mortality and what it means. And while we are here, we have a spiritual mission to perform. I have seen miracles of healing and fighting out on the frontier among the Apache that people back east could never begin to understand. It's the spirit power that does it. We all have it. It's a question of claiming it and using it. Right now, unless we can change the beliefs of the Southern states about slavery, then the South is doomed. Appealing to the Christian belief system in the Southern culture is the key to changing the state's belief in the necessity of slavery. The Creator God made all people to be free. To put people containing the divine spark of the Creator into bondage is an insult to the Creator's image, glory, and limitless bounty. We have high-ranking generals in the Southern army who know this to be true. My friend General Jackson has for years spent substantial sums of his own personal money to teach the Christian religion to slave children. He prays every night for the families of slaves and their protection. You'll see, Al, that the things I speak of are coming to pass now. And we, the Southern generals, will make these things happen for the good of our great nation that will soon be a reality."

"I don't doubt your word, General. You and your ways are a mystery to me, but your immense victories speak for themselves. I, along with my men, will continue to follow you to the North or to the gates of hell if need be."

"Thanks for your pledge, General Pike. I may have to hold you to it."

As we were concluding our discussion, General Beauregard arrived. "General Worth, I have received orders from Richmond. I have been relieved of command in the west and will take a new assignment in the east to oversee and construct new fortifications at Richmond. You are to assume overall command here of the Army of Mississippi as well as your Army of the Trans-Mississippi and the two they have combined to be named the Army of the West. They have also promoted you to general-in-chief, effective immediately. From now on, you will be getting your orders directly from Richmond. Congratulations on a much deserved promotion and your new command! What are your plans now?"

"Well, sir, I have spent all day here writing up an operation plan for the invasion of Kentucky. I propose to move the army out of Nashville by the end of the month. I want the men to spend the next ten days getting this area cleaned up and organized and making the whole city into a military base. After that, seeing that the Union Army is nonexistent in this theater, the only thing that can slow down a rapid invasion of the North is us outrunning our supply system. But at some point we will be transitioning to acquiring supplies from the North, which we will turn into our host. But the most critical of our supplies, which

I am patiently waiting for, are the special ordnance and ammunition on their way up from Texas right now. I have instructed my gunsmiths to send their production equipment along with their latest lot of production. We will need the equipment much closer to the front. Shipment takes too long from Texas. We will set up the equipment here in the shops we are building in Nashville. We should have enough smoke ordnance and cartridges for the special artillery in another week or so to take along with us when we march north."

"Where are you going to strike first, General?"

"I will strike Cincinnati, Ohio, first. That will be the first target in the North. The fall of Cincinnati will be like a thunderbolt that will bring this war home to the haters of the South who go about their daily business as if they didn't have a care in this world. They will soon have much to care about other than stuffing war profits into their wallets and consuming delicacies that are now out of the reach of their Southern cousins. Nevertheless, I doubt it will change the course of the actions now unfolding in Virginia. That plan is too far advanced for anything to change it. We must pray that our superior leadership will prevail in turning back that monstrosity of an invasion force."

"General, you think that an offensive war is the only solution? This puts you at odds with the gentlemen at Richmond who think that the war is simply a series of pistol duels and all we have to do to win is outduel the opponent."

"General, I get your irony. Who gets to referee this game and declare the winner?" I asked with a laugh. "You know as well as I, General, once this game turns into the war of attrition, we lose. It doesn't matter what the score is up until then. We must invade as quickly as possible. We must strip their cities of all the sinews of industry and wait for our chance to strike the killing blow to their armies. Thankfully, God has blessed us with generals like yourself, Jackson, Johnston, Lee, and Longstreet who fully understand what I am talking about. With regard to Cincinnati, I will do as Caesar did to Carthage and lace the ground with salt so that it will never again be a city of any value to an army. I am hoping that when the hue and cry goes up from all the unprotected cities of the North, the rail-splitter will have no choice but to react. Maybe he will raise a new army that we can defeat. That is my hope. My special artillery will gather them in for delivery to the next world like a farmer gathers in his wheat before the scythe."

"General Worth, I must warn you about disclosing any plans for devastating a Northern city to President Davis and the other gentlemen of the government. Such a thing would go against their unspoken rule against making war on innocent civilians."

"Oh, I am all too aware of the catastrophic nature of the Southern gentleman's honor code. I have conducted a study of it over the years and have credited it with precipitating this unnecessary war to begin with. I will definitely leave that part out of any operations plan I forward onto Richmond. When innocent civilians are forced from their homes, I will say that it couldn't be helped. I may even pay off those who complain with the latest Confederate currency as reparations. But in the meantime, the march of my army further into the North will strike such fear in the local people that they will be willing to pressure their politicians to clamor for the rail-splitter to accept and sign any terms of peace to get our Southern leviathan out of their state. Only a large-scale outpouring of pain in the Northern cities will bring this war to a quick end. If you leave this war in the hands of the Southern gentlemen, then the war will go on and on until the last Southern soldier fires the last defective, underpowered bullet from the last Southern granddad's long rifle. And the South will be so devastated that if a bird wishes to fly over its land, it will have to carry its own food. Is my analysis correct, General?"

"I am afraid your analysis is correct, General Worth."

General Beauregard and I spoke long into the night. He finally went back to his camp at one in the morning.

The next day, a beautiful spring sun arose. It was the nineteenth of April, the day of the Battles of Lexington and Concord in 1775. For the first time the world had seen a government that was based on natural law, not the law of a tyrant. What was important was that a group of men, our forefathers, had planted the seed of freedom, even if that seed would have to grow among the weeds. That seed would indeed grow and push away the weeds and one day tower over them to absorb all the light and make those weeds dry up and disappear. But instead of government by natural law, we had a new tyranny that wanted to devour part of itself whole. This war represented a rare opportunity for history. We could create two great democracies that the blood of their valiant dead purified to create a purer form of law, more just and benevolent than any seen before on the planet. Like Romulus and Remus, suckled by the wolf, these democracies would grow to become champions of law, justice, and truth. The pain was necessary to produce this historic uplifting.

We had clear telegraph communications from Nashville to Richmond. A little past midday, a message came through telling us to expect a visit from President Davis, who was on his way via rail. I had been wondering about the change of command. It appeared that President Davis had decided to implement it with a formal meeting. I was grateful for not having to make a trip to Richmond because I was very busy with plans for the upcoming movement. But I could imagine that the president was no less busy, given that almost a quarter million men were invading Virginia at this moment. I now had access to firsthand details of that enormous fight. The enemy was attacking Joe Johnston on the Yorktown Peninsula and also down the Shenandoah Valley. Perhaps Davis thought it best to come out and visit us now before the Richmond area became too hot to venture away from. I was anxious to hear if anything we had achieved out here was taking the pressure off of the capital. There was no indication of this. Even though the events that had taken place out here in the west had been an unmitigated disaster for Washington, they were, nevertheless, all happening on Southern territory. As long as that status did not change, then the events were an obscurity for the public in the North. Southern newspapers had been singing the praises of the Army of the West whereas Northern papers seemed subdued, not yet ready to sound the alarm bells. What they didn't know was that the audacity of the plans that I had made would unleash all hell on them. I was hoping that pressure from the invasion would cause priorities to change in Washington and bleed off the armies that were now tormenting Virginia. If we could defeat those armies, then we would be able to close the pincers on Washington and bring the rail-splitter to the negotiating table, hat in hand.

I spent the next three days trying to track down my special weapons supplies. Thanks to my unlimited use of the telegraph facilities here in Nashville, I was able to get word back of their location on the border of Arkansas on the way to Memphis, where they could go by rail the rest of the way. So we would soon be in possession of sufficient quantities of Gatling cartridges and smoke artillery to carry on with our modern warfare methods in the next round of the war. We were also getting the necessary machinery brought up for production here. I estimated the arrival time to be one more week at most. I would be issuing orders for the army to move immediately after receipt of those items.

The army at this time was in fine shape. They were well fed, well shod, well armed, and clean. I had emphasized personal hygiene over the last few days in my orders. Every single bucket and metal barrel capable of handling boiling water had been pressed into service for a nonstop campaign to delouse, disinfect, and deodorize the men. Not only would they feel better and look better, but the resultant restoration of sanitary conditions also would pay dividends in less sickness and higher morale. Some outfits had acquired shaving and barbering gear, allowing them their first haircuts and first opportunity for clean-shaven faces in months. As a result, they all looked better, smelled better, and felt better.

On the twenty-third, we learned by wire that the president had come through Chattanooga and after an overnight ride would arrive here in Nashville on the twenty-fourth. I was still in my tent headquarters here on Lawrence Hill. The time had finally come for me to screw up my courage to meet him in Nashville and face the crowds of people who had showered such affection on the men. I was sure Davis would want to address those crowds. I was hoping to not have to do likewise because I had never perfected the Southern accent. I hoped my duties would consist of no more than waving and smiling. I had always respected the divide between the politician and the soldier and looked at them as two entirely different callings. Besides, a Southern politician I would never be, not being able to speak the lingo.

On the twenty-third I had another late-night session with General Pike. He arrived at my tent with a Cherokee medicine man. "General Worth, do you mind if my friend and I keep you company for a while tonight?"

"It's my pleasure, General."

"This is Gawonii of the Cherokee. He fought with great ferocity at Pea Ridge."

"Greetings, Gawonii, and may I ask if you have your sacred pipe and tobacco so that we can smoke from it?"

"Yes, he has it, General. I told him that is what you like to do with your Indian friends," Pike interjected.

"It is a great honor to be here with the chief of the Southern Nation," Gawonii said.

"Well, I am a chief of the army but not the Southern Nation. The chief of the Southern Nation will be here tomorrow. I would like to sit with you and smoke. I will wait for you while you conduct the pipe-filling ceremony."

Gawonii pulled the two halves out of a long pouch and prayed as he screwed the halves together. He then blessed the tobacco and requested the presence of the spirits from the directions of the compass to witness the discussion and lend us their wisdom. He reverently filled the pipe and lit it from a twig that he had dipped into our campfire. Then we smoked from the living sacred pipe.

"How are things with your warriors, Gawonii?"

"The Creator is kind to us now. Most of the wounded warriors are healed. They all believe that under the great war chief Worth, we will be home soon at our own campfires with many tales of the battles we have fought in the great war. We are now engaged in a mission of war, but we know the great war chief will end this soon, and we will have great pride in being part of that victory. Does the great war chief think we will be secure in our homes under the new government?"

"Gawonii, the great father of the South will be here tomorrow. He is not ungrateful for your sacrifices and those of the great nations that have fought for our cause so well. And I can promise you that as long as I wear this uniform, I will never cease being a true friend of those in the territories and beyond. It was an unjust act of the chiefs of the North, what they did against your people by uprooting them and forcing them to live in a faraway land. That will not happen to you or your family again. Never again will you face exile in your own land. That was the product of the Northern money men and their greed, something our people in the

South have had to face and are fighting against. We fight to be left alone in our homeland also. You and your people will always have a special place at the dinner table of the South, and Southern teachers will teach Southern children about your noble deeds in this war for generations to come."

Gawonii passed me the sacred pipe, from which I took a long, satisfying draw.

"How are the Southern chiefs different from the Northern ones?" he asked.

I replied, "The Southern chiefs in the military are all of one mind. We are determined that all the corruption that has plagued our own people, we will put a stop to, and truth, righteousness, and virtue will finally prevail over our society. You are not our subordinates but our brothers-in-arms."

"What about our black brothers? What is to happen to them?"

"The Southern chiefs are in agreement," I said. "Our people believe in Jesus Christ, and he treated all men as equals. We will go ahead with our plans to restore brotherhood and sisterhood to all who live in the South. I myself am not a Christian, but I agree with them. The Creator has invested all with the divine spark of light; it exists in all. The law of the Creator governs all in the universe, and those who corrupt that law must pay a price. Right now the Southern Nation is drenching itself in the blood of its soldiers who have died at the hands of the Northern invader. This, I believe, is just punishment because the South believed in unjust laws. Likewise, the North has met with disaster here in the west because of its unjust invasion of the sacred soil of the South. The sacred hoop of first friendship is forever broken between the two nations due to mutual violation of the Creator's laws. Perhaps someday time will restore it, perhaps not. Perhaps after our soldiers shed enough of their blood, that will pay off the blood debt, and there will be peace again."

"It is good that one so powerful is also one who is wise in the ways of the Creator. I will sing a medicine song of healing for you and our warriors." With that, Gawonii sang a Cherokee song, simple and ancient as all his songs were.

I closed my eyes and felt the goodness of the earth come over me. I could feel the generations of good and noble Cherokee sending wave after wave of healing energy. When Gawonii had finished his song, I felt warm inside and at peace, in contrast to the feelings of pain that I had experienced upon witnessing so much death just a few days ago.

General Pike and Gawonii left me around midnight. I had a long day ahead tomorrow and a meeting with a man whom I both loved and feared. I loved President Davis for his gentlemanly nature and demeanor and feared him because he was a product of the Old South that needed to go away. I resolved to cajole him, flatter him—whatever it took to make him feel respected and obeyed even though I knew parts of him were in error and he did not resemble a lot of what I had just told Gawonii he did. He was, after all, the chief of the Southern gentlemen and was an embodiment of the Southern honor code. But he didn't know any better. I, on the other hand, not being a Southern gentleman, could see his deficiencies and those others of his government a mile off, and I had to constantly check my speech when in their presence. I really detested, for instance, their tradition of dueling when they came to disagreements. It was such a childish habit, not worthy of reasonable men and a costly habit too. But I had embraced the Southern people despite all their flaws, and it was far too late in the game to think any differently now. I guess I had a case of true love for a people and their society. I lay down and closed my eyes on my spartan army cot with these thoughts in my head and with the thought that tomorrow could be my greatest battle yet.

On the morn of the twenty-fourth, I slept in late, to around 9:30 a.m. I had left no orders the night before regarding when the duty officer was to wake me up, having decided to let nature take its course. I felt very refreshed by the extra sleep, which had cleared most of the cobwebs in my mind from the stress of the last few weeks. I ordered up a pot of Northern coffee and went over the evening's division reports. For breakfast I had a box of insect-free Northern hard crackers.

At noon a courier from town arrived and said that President Davis was waiting for me in a private railway car inside the city. So I jumped on my horse and headed to the train station, where I had placed an army band the day before. I had also placed twenty-one artillery pieces at the ready for the obligatory salute. I had ordered them to fire and the band to play simultaneously the moment I came within sight of the president. On the outskirts of town, people came out to cheer, unfortunately blocking my way. I would have to wade through the throng since they all wanted to take a look at the strange warrior from the North who had come to save them all from his peers.

It wasn't until one o'clock that I came in sight of the train station. As the president appeared from his car, having just finished a lunch, the band started playing, and the cannons started booming. As I finally rode up to the president's car, Davis waved and showed me a broad smile, which I had not thought he was capable of but which immediately put me at ease. I dismounted my horse in front of the honor guard, marched over to Davis, snapped to attention, and saluted him. He offered his hand, which I grabbed and shook with both of my hands. Then Davis gestured me to the side, where we both waved to a delighted crowd. I was unsure whether Davis would address the crowd. After five minutes with the crowd, which was now frantic with adulation, Davis grabbed me by the arm and took me into his passenger car.

"Good afternoon, General Worth. Your soldiers look in fine shape and great spirits."

"Yes, sir. They have been polishing and brushing all week. It has been a real morale boost to march the streets of Nashville in parade. I have made sure all regiments have gotten the chance."

"That is terrific, General, and I want to say how full of pride the nation and my government are for the magnificent job you have done here in the west by completely sweeping the Northern armies from our land. God bless you, General. Your efficiency and economy of force have been breathtaking to behold, something your renowned father would fully embrace with pride were he still alive to witness it."

"How long are you to be with us, sir?"

"I am only here to see you for a few hours, to go over some things with you personally. Then I have to immediately proceed back to Richmond. As you know from our telegraph dispatches, our armies are fully engaged on the peninsula and in the Shenandoah Valley, where your old chum Jackson is in command, God protect him. I have only this short time to talk with you here in the railcar; then I must head back."

"I'm sorry to hear that, sir. I was hoping you could stay a few days and get to see the whole army."

"Thank you, General. If it weren't for that Northern accent of yours, I would swear you were a Southerner by your hospitality. Please pardon me for my abrupt change of subject, but there are some items I wish to go over with you. First of all, this new gun that you have invented—my staff have told me that it is good only as a defensive weapon. What do you say to that?"

"Well, Mr. President, I did not invent the gun. I have simply invented some tactics for use of that gun. Any new weapon might be useless if the appropriate tactics are not employed. And with all due respect to your staff, I have proven them quite wrong here in the battle for this city. My artillery crews have demonstrated that a massed concentration of firepower on a narrow front with these guns will chew a hole right through the enemy line. The guns can move forward using a bounding and covering technique until they are in position for maximum lethality to the enemy line. We can do this to a point where any enemy soldier who lifts his head to fire will be shot immediately. I have no doubt that this gun with this high rate of fire would also work extremely well in defense against a massed concentration of soldiers in the open. But this is not how I choose to employ it. I am not here to defend anything. I am here to attack."

"That's precisely my point, General. My staff and I have to know what your intentions are now. What are your immediate plans for the army now that you have met your objectives in the west?"

"Well, sir, General Beauregard and I have proposed that our next objective should be the liberation of Kentucky."

"Splendid, General. And because of the rapidity of your victories, we need to know, what might be your plans after that? At the rate you are going, Kentucky will fall in a few weeks. What are your plans after that?"

"Mr. President, after the liberation of Kentucky, we will have the opportunity to take the fight to the North and give them a taste of what they have been giving us. We think a thrust into Ohio may help relieve the pressure from our army in the east. Perhaps Lincoln will shift large numbers of his army to protect the west. So far he has not responded to our victories whatsoever but is solely committed to attacking the South and threatening Richmond. We may even have the opportunity to march east ourselves and combine for a joint attack on Washington, depending on the enemy reaction."

"General, you have my approval for this move into the north on a few conditions. I have already made an enormous increase in your power by giving you the overall command. I have invested a great deal of trust in you by doing this. But first of all, there has been great disturbance at the stories of your Indian soldiers scalping and desecrating the bodies of the enemy soldiers. Is that true? If so, that must stop, and you must promise me that it will never happen again!"

"Well, sir, you have to understand that in their first engagement at Pea Ridge, those soldiers had not yet been indoctrinated in the laws of warfare of the Southern army, and I am afraid their exuberance over their former antagonists got the better of them. I have instructed General Pike that such a breach of discipline will never be tolerated again. In our battle here in Nashville, there was not a single case of this behavior to the best of my knowledge."

"That's good, General, because I must warn you that if it does take place again, there will be severe repercussions for you and your men."

"You have my word, sir—no such breeches of discipline will happen again."

"As you know, General, the Northern newspapers have exploited this issue to propagandize and dishonor the entire Southern army by claiming that we are all war criminals. That's why this must never happen again."

"Understood, sir!"

"Also, you must avoid damage to civilians in the upcoming foray into Ohio. Our fight is not against civilians, but against the military and the leadership of the North."

"Understood, sir!"

"Very good, General. This has been an easy meeting. I am very pleased with you, your performance, and your men. Will you join me for a short meeting with some of my staff members? After that I must make my way back to Richmond. And before I forget, congratulations on your promotion to general-in-chief. Never before has such a promotion been earned in the history of warfare!"

"Thank you so much, Mr. President, for your kind words."

With that we walked into an adjacent railcar, and Davis introduced me to members of his staff for a series of short discussions. I left the president's train at three o'clock. As the band struck up Dixie, the president smiled and waved. The train whistle sounded, and off he went.

I had promised the president that I would not do damage to civilians, which included their property, but the truth was that once the army crossed over into the North, it would burn a huge swath through Ohio and destroy everything of military value, and unfortunately, a lot of civilian property would be mixed in with it. There would be no avoiding it. I didn't have the heart to tell him that, nor did I want him to strip me of command. Politicians needed to stick to their jobs, and soldiers had to stick to theirs.

For the next few days the army spent all of its time taking stock of itself. My instructions were for the men to rest and eat as much as they could over the next week. They were to get themselves ready for what I had planned to be the final leg of the war. We were getting new recruits by ones and twos, as well as whole units up to regiment strength. They were coming in from all parts of the South. I came to appreciate the difficulties of supplying and feeding upward of 80,000 men. They were consuming two million full rations a week. And I told them to eat everything they could get their hands on to get up their strength. We were getting trains from the Southern heartland by rail, which provided us with about half of what we needed. The other half came from supplies that we had seized and from the locals who provided us with herds of livestock— chickens and hogs mostly. Much came as a donation from farmers who wanted to contribute to the war. But I knew that this supply was not bottomless. I figured that after two more weeks, this middle Tennessee area's surplus would be tapped out. If we didn't move on by then, we would begin to be a hardship on the local sources. For the time being, however, the men were savoring abundant feasts. Morale was at its highest. The men took pride in their appearance once again. Gone for the time being was that sunken-faced scarecrow look of tired, hungry, ragged, and foul-smelling soldiery.

The Southern soldiers had a well of wisdom about them and a special tenacity that the Northern soldiers lacked. Southerners loved the charge and the attack in battle. They felt uncomfortable being penned up in trenches. That's why they liked my command. I could let them fight battles the way they liked to achieve victory. But even though I considered myself a military visionary, I also considered myself incredibly lucky that so far all my plans had worked out. The biggest gift I had received from the gods of war was the timing of my arrival with my corps on the battlefield at Shiloh. Not only had the timing been perfect, but the location and direction that we had arrived from had been perfect too. We had inserted ourselves to the rear of the enemy at a time when both sides had fought to a standstill and the Southern commander was dead. Our fortunate timing had nothing to do with me. That was a God-given opportunity that was completely accidental, not the result of any genius of mine. But I would admit that to no one. Let the soldiers keep thinking that I had planned it. That way they would fight the future battles without worries. This psychological edge that we had gotten from that battle made us all look ten feet tall. I was very humbled to have defeated a truly talented adversary in General Thomas and to have taken him prisoner. My Army of the Trans-Mississippi, God had truly blessed.

My tent out on Lawrence Hill had now grown to many tents and a fully equipped operations center. We had had linemen run telegraph wires to it and now got information from all over the South. Every day we sent out scouting parties and received others coming in. We were patching together the situations in Ohio and Kentucky. The picture that my staff was getting showed that confusion reigned there. Washington had done little more than send out engineering officers to different cities to design and construct defensive fortifications. The enemy knew that a storm was brewing. They knew that in a few short weeks our army would be coming north to unleash hell and that they were mostly defenseless. Washington was totally committed to its offensive on Richmond and was not going to change course. The Northerners were oblivious to the coming crisis for them in the western theater. No doubt, they had a three-to-one manpower advantage in the east. If things went bad there, Davis would order us to move east. That's why we had to move quickly out here and be ready for the call, should it come.

Our cavalry would be even more important to us than ever in the move north. They would have to fan out over the North in foraging operations to locate and procure new sources of food and supplies as we got farther away from our Southern sources. General Forrest was in command of a large force now, almost 20,000 mounts. I had a talk with the general about many things not necessarily related to the army. I wanted to know about his personality and frame of mind. It was an interesting, far-reaching discussion.

"General Forrest, I want you to know that I have petitioned Richmond for your promotion to major general, and you will most likely have it by the time we move out."

"I am honored, General," Forrest replied.

"General, I know that while the army is standing down for the time being in Nashville, your men have not been able to. We have kept them busy on extensive scouting missions, but I do want them to get the food and the rest they need. I don't want them to feel oppressed or overly burdened."

"Oh, don't worry about that, General. My men love what you have done and will ride to the ends of the earth if you tell them to."

"Thank your men for placing their faith in me."

"General, my men think that you have been able to engineer these victories because you know how the Yankees think and know better than any one of us how to whip them. We thank God for such leadership. Just keep pointing us in the right direction, and we will keep driving the Yankees hard."

"General Forrest, we need to talk about specifics. My staff has briefed you on the main objective. We are to invade Kentucky and push on up into Ohio. This army will move in a fortnight, right after we have replenished our military ordnance fully. We are also getting a large shipment of Confederate script. We will be getting several wagonloads of that, and it will be placed in your custody. We will pay for everything in enemy territory that we seize. Your foraging parties will be what feeds our army once we get north of the border. I will still be requesting military supplies from our forward base here in Nashville, but everything else—food, forage, and everything we consume daily—is going to be coming from our hosts. I know it will be a burden to you, but Richmond is demanding an accounting of everything we take and the money that gets paid out. You need to assign a clerk to every one of the foraging parties and make sure they record dates, times, and places and how much money gets paid out and for what. It is up to these clerks to make it clear to the Northern farmers that they will be subject to military justice if they refuse to sell their stock and products to us. Penalties will be up to and including forfeiture of property upon conviction. Our tribunal will execute summary judgments on the spot, and there will be no appeals. Any towns or facilities you find of significant military significance must be reported to my staff immediately. This includes any shop, factory, or forge that provides military supplies or anything of potential military value. Most likely, I will issue an order of immediate destruction of such facilities."

"Understood, sir!"

"Do you have any questions?"

"No, sir. It is all very clear."

"Now that I have gone over my official instructions, which Richmond has demanded that I do, I would like the rest of this conversation to be strictly off the record. Richmond has warned me to play this game in a manner according to the unspoken laws of chivalry and decorum, and I have agreed to do so to put their minds at ease. I must tell you, however, that we are in a new age of total war. The rules of chivalry will lose us the Southern homeland— the Southern Nation, General. This is the reality that you and I have to face. My generals are not the round-table knights, and I am not King Arthur, and this is not merry old England. The sooner we all realize this, the better. Do you understand what I am saying, General Forrest?"

"I do, sir."

"Very well then. Having said this, I don't want your men to feel constrained from doing what they feel they need to do for the good of our efforts. I don't want you to hold back from any threats, and if you see something that might threaten us, put it to the torch first; then get with my staff on it later. Are you hearing me, General?"

"Yes, sir. It is music to my ears."

"General, I know that we will most likely overstep our bounds, but ultimately, I will have to be the one who answers for it to Richmond ... Now on a more personal note, General Forrest, I want to sound you out on what caused this insane war in the first place—slavery. You were a slave trader before the war. What is your attitude toward the slaves?"

"General, it was just a business to me. I was a businessman just like any other. I never thought much about it. This was the society I was born into, and this was the business that I knew. As far as the good or evil of it, it's evil, of course.

There were many injustices committed against the slave folk. I know it, and I saw it with my own eyes. I tried not to be one of those unscrupulous traders who broke up families or allowed them to be sent to masters with a reputation for cruelty. I would not do that. I grew up with slave folk, and I have many friends among them. I surround myself with my most trusted fighters, who are sons of slaves. You know that for generations, our slaves were happy with us, as we were with them. That all changed with the cotton trade. The slaves on the cotton plantations got worked to death, and it seemed nothing could stop it because there was too much money involved. And a lot of that money went to finance the damned Yankee government that started this here war. And they sent their overseers and tariff collectors down here to see that money got paid. And all the time, more money went to them. It was never enough. And at the same time we had the Yankee abolitionists spreading their hatred against us. They insulted and threatened us at the same time as they picked our pockets. And the ones who paid the price were the slave folk. I hate the money-grubbing Yankees and what they have done to us. They have turned our noble society into a den of thieves and money-grubbers. And they hate us for what they have turned us into."

"General Forrest, what would you say if I asked you if it was time to free the slaves? Would you accept that notion?"

"General Worth, after all that has happened, I don't see how we can possibly go back to the institution of slavery. As far as why it came about in the first place and why it still exists, it's a mystery to me. I say end it and be done with it forever. I say the sooner we are done with it, the quicker we get all the meddling Yankees down here off of our soil for good."

"General Forrest, I am glad we discussed this, and I can tell you we are of the same mind, along with others of our military leaders back east. The time will come when we have to stand with stout hearts against those elements in our society, many of them in the aristocracy, the Southern gentlemen class—we will have to stand up against them and not back down in our demand for a permanent end to this corrupt institution that is undermining our society. We will talk on this subject again. In the meantime I will keep you updated on our preparations to move out. Please prepare your men and animals as best as you can. You will have the most active role to play in the upcoming fight. Take good care of yourself, General."

"Don't worry about me, sir. I am like the cat who has nine lives. I am only up to the third, I reckon."

It wasn't until May 1 that the shipment of cartridges and smoke ordnance arrived on the train from Texas along with the machinery that would produce the ammunition at this newfound base in Nashville. Work crews, including builders and carpenters from all of the four corps present, constructed a huge new complex of buildings and warehouses in the shortest period of time to create the new base. Supplies had been piling up for the first time in substantial quantities. My guess was that these supplies would be used to outfit recruits and new formations since most of the men in this army had grown comfortable in their existing clothing and accoutrements. More men than I was aware of traded in their ropes and old belt buckles, preferring to stick with the SN theme.

Finally, the move-out day arrived. It was May 7 when the order went out to all four corps commanders as well as Forrest's reinforced corps of cavalry. The infantry corps commanders were Hardee, Bragg, Polk, and Breckenridge. My old Trans-Mississippi Army and the Texans were now attached to Breckenridge. His would now be the largest of the four corps, with five and a half divisions, followed by Bragg's with five. The army had kept the new designation as well—the Army of the West. With new recruits and new formations coming in, it had mushroomed to some 90,000 men at last muster. We had surplus rifles and weaponry to arm another 40,000 if the opportunity came. Whether or not the citizenry of Kentucky would commit to our cause was a wild card. But the momentum in the war had definitely swung our way, so the prospects of a successful recruitment drive in Kentucky looked good since we were coming to stay as a governing force, not just as an army.

We crossed into Kentucky on the tenth of May. We marched through Bowling Green on the twelfth. From there we would follow parallel to the rail line heading up to Louisville, thus maintaining easy communication and transport with our Nashville base. So far there had been no opposition, not even a skirmish. We passed by abandoned fortifications along the way. Our cavalry patrols reported nothing between Bowling Green and Louisville. On the thirteenth, I ordered Forrest north with his corps, to take Louisville. Word got back to us on the sixteenth that Forrest's corps had taken Louisville unopposed. I decided to shuttle the Army of the West up the rail line into Louisville. By the twentieth the entire Army of the West was on station in Louisville. From there I sent a detached brigade from Breckenridge's corps by rail to occupy Frankfort and to put out the call to all the military-aged men to come to the city and take up arms for the cause.

We sent up enough surplus arms to Frankfort to equip a whole corps. However, we were not going to loiter in the area long enough to get the forces organized so they could join us. At the moment we had all we could handle of new men who were untested in combat. My operations plan was to send Forrest's cavalry up into Indiana, seize rail lines, make a feint toward Indianapolis, and then turn east to the main objective Cincinnati.

Chapter 5

Cincinnati

We would able to move very fast once Forrest seized the rail lines that we needed. Then we could move the whole army via rail lightning-fast without the soldiers having to sacrifice shoe leather, which at this point was pretty much irreplaceable unless we seized it from the enemy supply houses. Other items in short supply were tents, blankets, and uniforms. These stocks were completely inadequate because the South still had not enough industrial base; it had had virtually none before the war, and nothing really had changed much. I saw that the army in the east was marching around with a substantial percentage of the formations shoeless and in rags. I had done my very best to avoid that here, but if it weren't for all the matériel that we had seized from the commissary stores of the three captured armies, then our boys would be suffering the same fate as the boys back east. Travel by rail saved a lot on the wear and tear of a march and, more importantly, was lightning-fast. I was sure that the rail-splitter in Washington had no idea of what we were going to do, where we were going at present, or our numbers.

The further north we penetrated, the more extensive became the rail network. We had a solid, secure line all the way to Nashville, where our engineers had conducted a crash program in constructing a huge rail yard with the capability of receiving numerous cars and stacking them into trains. We accumulated railcars and engines in large quantities, assembled them, and sent them out in trains that could carry whole regiments and divisions of men at a time. It was turning into a logistical marvel, and every rail line was like a great sword pointed at the heart of the enemy. We could threaten a city and then attack from a completely different direction with no need to concentrate or coordinate far-flung formations over a vast expanse or worry about old maps and phantom trails. Our formations were able to offload and form a line of battle virtually within an hour after arrival. Moreover, the men could catch some sleep along the way and not be worn out from marching. They would be fully aware and refreshed when it came time for battle. In this phase of the war, I discovered the beauty and efficiency of army movement via rail.

On the twenty-third, word came back from cavalry patrols that the rail lines all the way to Indianapolis were clear. Our Northern spy network also told us that the rail lines were clear in all zones. "Clear, clear, clear" was all that we were getting. Where was the enemy resistance? There seemed to be vast confusion among the enemy about how to prepare for the coming showdown. Would anyone from the North make a stand? The cities in our theater, according to our spies, were in a full-blown panic. Mayors and city authorities were making the decisions, not Northern army officers. Businesses were reluctant to shut down and let their workers form into citizen armies. The militias that had formed were little more than mobs with weapons run by local constabulary. They were frantically drilling and trying to absorb the basics of soldiering, led by non-soldiers. The presence of federal soldiers was very slim. Governor Robinson of Kentucky had fled his state with a small force to join Governor Todd of Ohio. The general in charge of the defense of Cincinnati was Major General Horatio Wright, who was commanding the so-called Army of Ohio, a command that existed only on paper. Moreover, Wright had spent all of his time with the citizen labor crews constructing fortifications and rifle pits south of the Ohio River, expecting the main blow to come overland from northern Kentucky. He clearly had made no provisions nor expected a strike coming from the west via rail. It became obvious to me that the entire western half of the so-called Union was in the air. My reconnaissance forces were probing all over the area of operations and were finding nothing in the way of any significant organized resistance. All seemed to be chaos.

We now had 80,000 effective infantry and a beefed-up force of 20,000 cavalry, almost twice the strength of our army in the east. Evidently, Forrest's recruitment campaign in Kentucky had attracted a lot of young men with mounts. And life in the saddles was more fun than trudging through the dirt on foot. If only TJ could have seen the force that I had, he would be astonished.

We were now at the end of May, and the time to make our move had finally come. All rail lines were secure with our soldiers. We had all the trains assembled and stacked at the switching yards back in Nashville, awaiting the order to move. Once the officers got those orders, the empty trains would race up the Louisville and Nashville railroad. From there, the army with all its gear would board for a ride up two sets of tracks heading to Indianapolis. Then they would divert to a track heading to Cincinnati. From there, they would offload on the western outskirts of the city. We would then send the divisions out in echelon on a giant arc around the north of the city. Once the encirclement was complete, I would attack the high ridges to the north and rush my five hundred cannons, all lined hub to hub along the ridge. Then would come a firepower demonstration with cannons firing incendiary and solid shots down on the city. Then I would order all incendiary rounds for the artillerymen to fire. I would accept a peaceful surrender of the city at any time. My guess was that the commanding general of the city, whoever that might be, would request a ceasefire to evacuate the citizens of the city. There would be no escape because the city would be in between my men and the Ohio River.

On the night of May 27, I issued the orders. The assembly area in Nashville disgorged itself of all the empty trains. Long trains with multiple locomotives whisked their way up the Louisville and Nashville rail line. By morning they had all arrived. The day of the twenty-eighth, 80,000 men and all their equipment loaded onto the trains. The cars were packed. Men rode in the cars and on the roofs of the cars. Not all the men and equipment made it aboard, but most did. My prayer that day was that no one would fall off and be hurt. The night of the twenty-eighth, the move was on. The trains first traveled up the tracks to Indianapolis in a feint and then made the switch to the Cincinnati-bound track as we had planned. Cavalry pickets screened us along the way. Amazingly, there was not even a single skirmish, right up to the objective. What little resistance there was, a few odd rifle shots, Forrest's men swept away. The soldiers offloaded to the west of the city and were met by two brigades of Forrest's cavalry outside of Mill Creek. They quickly formed into regiments and divisions and began their march around the city, encountering a few uncoordinated and piecemeal attacks from the irregular citizen soldiers, or squirrel hunters as they called them. There were no significant fortifications north of the city because the military planners had never conceived of any threat coming from that direction. By noontime three of the four corps, three deployed, one still in transit, completed the encirclement. All cannons made it up the ridges shortly after 2:00 p.m. on the twenty-ninth. This was an extraordinary feat of pure determination. I sent orders that bombardment would commence at 3:00 p.m. The sporadic rifle fire from the squirrel hunters became more frequent. The citizens made a few massed charges against us. Little clumps of men seemed to gather or appear in front of the line, fire a volley, and then retreat after receiving a withering return volley. As it turned out, the Battle of Cincinnati wasn't really much of a battle.

At 3:00 p.m. our four to five hundred cannons—some were still coming into line—opened fire on the city. The heated-up cherry-red cannonballs quickly set dozens of little fires with each volley. Then the artillery commanders ordered the men to fire at will. Immediately, flames started shooting up from all directions as the multiple fires started to converge. After an hour's bombardment, I ordered a cease-fire. No white flag was evident. The city, however, was totally engulfed in flames that were devastating it. The citizens were crossing the Ohio River to safety on boats, barges, or anything that would float. We stood by as they fled.

The sky that night was a bright orange and red as the city went aflame from one side to the other. It was almost night turned into day by the light of the conflagration. The next day, the thirtieth, our army looked out in awe over the burned-out hulk of what used to be a great city. Fires were still burning, but the bloom of the great city was now all burned away. The inhabitants had all fled. It was a smokestack city now. All the buildings and wood were gone. Only burnt masonry and tall brick smokestacks stood to remind us of what used to be there. No one offered surrender. We heard from no mayor, no council, no representative, and no military authority. I guess my thought of being met by someone in authority who would beg us not to attack had been just a naive dream. I really hadn't expected this event. The casualties on our side were paltry, probably less than one hundred of a serious nature during the whole assault. We had struck the soft underbelly of the North, and the results were astounding. A city that had taken generations to build, an army of 100,000 men had destroyed in one night and almost entirely unintentionally. I was not sure if I was going to catch grief about this from Richmond. Although this was no doubt a great victory that would help shorten the war, no one celebrated in the eerie ruins. There was quiet among all the soldiers that bordered on melancholy. How awful war can be.

May 31 arrived, and we used the newly seized telegraph to send our requests back to Nashville for whatever rations they could send. We had to settle in and decide where our next strike would be. Orders came from Richmond for us to hold our position. This was not an order I was entirely happy with. But evidently, a lot was going on back east. General Joe Johnston had been seriously wounded, and overall command now fell to General Robert E. Lee. General Jackson was fighting armies twice and three times his size and somehow whipping the enemy in the Shenandoah Valley. It was possible that Davis wanted us to stop our independent invasion of the North and instead shoot across to march on Washington from the west. This might have been the rationale behind his last order. But he also might have wanted to use us as bait to lure away the massive force with which the North was invading Virginia. As soon as word got out that Cincinnati was no more, the pressure on Washington would be intense to do something. Should McClellan take Richmond, no doubt, Richmond would suffer the same fate.

But in the meantime, I had 100,000 adult male mouths to keep fed, and we would no longer be receiving herds of livestock from friendly natives only too happy to give them to us. From now on, we would have to confiscate our food and forage. Word came from Frankfort, Kentucky, that 30,000 men had now taken oaths to fight for the new government there. This was astounding. Our victories were bringing in huge numbers of recruits who wanted a piece of the action before it all was over. For the time being they would be a defensive army but would train offensively in case we needed them. We needed men to relieve our soldiers who were strung all up and down the rail lines that we had seized in Indiana and Ohio to defend them. Once the new Kentucky governor had authorized the new recruits to operate beyond state lines, therefore putting them under my jurisdiction, the rail lines were where I would be sending them—not glamorous work but very necessary. And my army could get back a lot of its seasoned veterans from such duty. They could be put back in their home units and would help strengthen unit integrity. We would be staying here several weeks by the look of things, given what was panning out in the east. We would do as we had in Nashville—namely, turn this city into a military base, including putting together rail-switching yards and assembly areas for the massing of railcars in preparation for the next great leapfrogging operation when we had to send the army off to another battle via rail. It took hundreds of cars to move this army, rifles and baggage in total. We had commandeered cars from all over the South—boxcars, passenger cars, flatbeds, locomotives—and now had great numbers from the rail yards of the North.

By far the busiest component of our army was the mounted component. Not only were they conducting raids, reconnaissance, feints, and all-out attacks, but now they also had foraging duties to perform among a disgruntled and hostile populace. We had adequate communication and transport from our southern base in Nashville, but the base could not meet more than a portion of our needs. We also sent out infantry units for foraging—those who were not busy on the engineering projects. We would send them out on the trains into the rural areas to scour the countryside in the hope of seeing them return with the trains fully loaded. We had enough Confederate script back in the city of Nashville to wallpaper the whole town, so I issued orders for it to be brought up. From our base here in Ohio, I thought it reasonable to believe that we would soon be sending mountains of food and matériel back down into the South and would give back all that we had taken and more.

If I had to stay here and hold this position, which might appeal to the gentlemen in Richmond but which was a terrible waste of an army, then that was not to say that we couldn't still create havoc all throughout this Northern theater and bleed them dry. I could keep army headquarters here, but nothing could stop me from sending out massive raiding parties and a reconnaissance in force. One such plan I began to develop was to send a division or two or even a corps up the rails to the city of Indianapolis, not to control the city but basically to loot it of all that was worth taking for the war effort. I didn't want a repeat of what had happened here in Cincinnati. A dead city was of no use to anybody, but a live city would have a lot of matériel that we needed not just here but in the South. The South desperately needed equipment, machines, steam engines, industrial items, tools, steel, and all kinds of parts and pieces that could be found in the cities of the North.

And whatever we could carry away, we could transport to all points in the South, via our large and growing rail network. The rail system, of course, was not so extensive in the South, but when we could get matériel to the various depots, transport could go overland from there and make it to all points eventually. I thought we had the opportunity to be a net supplier of goods, not a net consumer. That was my dream at the moment. That might make me sound more like a pirate and less like a general, but this army had a great opportunity, not strictly soldiering, and I was going to see that we wasted not a single man-hour sitting idle. We were not going to practice drill and ceremony all day when there was loot to be had and bases of supply we could construct to strengthen ourselves for future battle.

Our control over the midsection of the so-called Union continued unchallenged. This was an opportunity that had not existed for many armies in history. This war needed to be over soon, as I had told my staff and men at least a hundred times, because once it turned into a war of attrition, the South would lose. As our successes mounted, and as I conversed several times with various citizens of Ohio, I began to question whether their hearts were really in this war. I heard several of them express doubts and regrets and blame their politicians for the current catastrophe. Secretly, my heart ached for many of the people up here, the old and the humble who didn't really know what it was all about and wanted nothing but peace. Now their great city was nothing but ashes, and they were the victims of something they'd had no part in creating. Nevertheless, as soldiers we had a deadly job to do, and we would get it done so that this would not happen to our people or our cities, as it surely would if we failed in our mission.

A full week had passed since the order to hold this position. We had a new rail yard half-constructed as we worked around the clock in shifts. The Kentucky militia, now under my command, had fanned out on various rail lines and had secured the line going south from Cincinnati to Louisville. So we were sending and receiving trains on two lines now on a daily basis. It looked like Cincinnati would become another Nashville for us, in the territory of the enemy. It would become our forward military base. Foraging parties were now going out and bringing in supplies on a daily basis. The men were getting fed and getting fed well. Sanitation points were set up along the river, and we had plenty of boiled water. We had seen no activity from federal gunboats. There were no armies coming our way to confront us. It seemed that no general and no army, even if available, wanted to test our abilities and be swallowed whole like the three armies that had already faced us. We had become a frightening juggernaut, and Northern papers wildly overstated our numbers, some estimating our size at a quarter million men. If you counted all the militias we had recently absorbed and our main body, then you would get half that number. But it all worked in our favor. I didn't know who was coming up with the estimates for the North—some reports said it was the Pinkerton private detective agency—but this was all favorable to us.

In an effort to keep up with our myth of invincibility, I finished my plans to conduct a massive reconnaissance with a substantial portion of Forrest's cavalry—some 12,000 men—and a main body of 30,000 infantry, a heavily reinforced corps under Breckenridge. This would include my boys from the old Trans-Mississippi Army. They were my best soldiers at this point. Forrest would have his men do what they were quite used to by now: secure the rail line all the way to Indianapolis, take engineering soldiers with them who would repair or replace any sabotage to the line, then detach companies to guard bridges or any strategic points from enemy attack. Then I would send Breckenridge and his force up the line by rail. They would offload somewhere in the outskirts of the city, where they could assemble in line of battle and then strike at selected points that Forrest's scouts had identified as critical to control of the city. I would authorize Breckenridge to accept a ransom in gold for the pledge to not bombard the city as we had done in Cincinnati. Hopefully, he would find someone in authority to arrange for this transaction. If this could not be accomplished, then his orders would be to enter the city, take all that was militarily useful, and then prepare to torch the city once this was done. Accompanying him would be twelve Gatling guns since the army had just received a delivery of twelve more assembled from our gunsmith shops in Nashville. This would effectively offset any resistance by local militia.

Forrest and I worked out this plan together. June 14 was the date his force would move out. Breckenridge would assemble his force and stand by for the go order from Forrest. Our intelligence on the city of Indianapolis was poor. The further north we penetrated, the thinner the reliable information would get. It was a state capital.

That meant there would be a state arsenal, and a few of our agents reported foundries and armories that were producing cannons and ammunition. There were also various factories, manufacturing facilities, stockyards, warehouses, and depots closely connected to the rail hub.

Our experience in Cincinnati told us a lot about what we could expect. There would be some resistance, but for the most part, the city would be undefended. Whether or not there would be a complete collapse of the city into panic and chaos, with no contact between city officials and our attacking force, we could not know. I had fully expected that when we showed ourselves on the ridges of Cincinnati, someone would come forward, but no one did. Here we would try to seek out officials first and not attack as soon as we arrived. I was leaving the decision to attack the city up to Forrest. He would be the best judge of what we needed to do to maximize the profit of the mission for us. In the best-case situation, the mayor would allow us to confiscate the gold from the vaults of all the banks, in exchange for Confederate script, of course, and we could save the city. We could then go on a big shopping spree for what the South needed and what we needed to stay in the field, all for Confederate script. If all went well, we would leave the city virtually the way it had been before our arrival. In the worst-case situation, we would have another Cincinnati. A third possibility was that the citizens of the city might put it under the torch themselves, not wanting us to benefit in any way from our capture of it. But whatever the case, the official report going back to Richmond had to state that we were not making war on civilians, and it had to be plausible.

Sometimes I thought that Cincinnati had been planned as a great skedaddle. None of the leading citizens had come forward to save their city. They might have planned on putting it to the torch anyway, but our cannon fire saved them the trouble. We saw no white flags there. There was just a whirlwind of chaos.

We hoped for a different outcome in Indianapolis. I discussed in detail with Forrest what our objectives needed to be. I hoped that only a show of our presence would be enough for them to send out the white flag, without need for a firepower demonstration. Then we could send in the boxcars and flatbeds to pack up as much loot as we could find. Also, with tranches of Confederate script came a letter of official pass. This meant that if the citizens wanted, they could pass through the lines down to the Southern states to spend their money and bring back goods if they so desired. None would, of course, because the Northern government would not allow such a thing. But our money was good. We were not stealing anything and were giving market prices for what we took from private citizens. Any public or commercial property, or things of military value such as railroad supplies, rails, and railcars, we would declare contraband of war, seize outright, and send back South. I also discussed with Forrest my overall goals. The truth was we didn't have enough time to go after the major cities to the northwest of us—no time to hit St. Louis or Chicago. Richmond also had signaled this by ordering us to stay put for the moment. They might need us for a cross-country defense of Richmond. I agreed with this order for different reasons. I had my sights set on attacking Washington.

Though we didn't have the time to attack the northwestern cities, that wasn't to say that we didn't need all those rails and rolling stock to the north or the west of Indianapolis. So once the city surrendered, which God willing would happen, Breckenridge's corps would stack arms and take hammers and bars to the rails and stack the flatbeds high for transport down to Cincinnati until we had all that we needed, and then we would pass all surplus down the line to Nashville. What this army needed was to initiate the biggest scrap-iron operation in modern history. The South desperately needed whatever we could procure for them. We had to avoid catching the city on fire at all costs. There were so many variables to consider when taking a city. To take the city, get whatever was of military significance, and pull out, leaving it in one piece, would be the more humane solution, but that would be up to the citizens. If they resisted, then the humane approach might not happen. It was hard to predict what effect the events in Cincinnati would have on their decision. My hunch was that they would not want this for their city.

If anyone who is of a gentle, kind, or innocent nature gets this far in reading these memoirs, such a reader might be asking himself or herself what kind of person could be planning so casually the destruction of an entire city. All I can say in my defense is that this was all part of the logic of war. If we all lived in a world where war was unheard of, then this might be a legitimate question. But we don't live in such a world. It amuses me how none of polite society can be honest about this. As far as career military people are concerned, so few of us dare speak about the reality of war to the public. Instead we have to speak in hushed tones and live a lie. We show up at public functions in our best uniforms, with polished brass, fancy sashes, gold-braided shoulder boards, engraved sabers, and foppish accoutrements, like toy soldiers out of a child's fairy-tale book. How dare we look like anything else? How dare we speak the truth of the realities of war? We are but toy soldiers in a grand toy-soldier army. The reality, of course, is so different. In reality all the soldier cares about is staying warm, staying out of the mud as much as possible, getting a square meal, and doing his best to accomplish his duty and at the same time live to see another day and not end up in a mass grave.

Was Genghis Khan an evil man? That I don't know, but I doubt it. He was simply a man who thoroughly understood the logic of war for his time. His scientific weaponry at that time was the Mongolian horseman, who could cover over one hundred miles a day fighting on horseback. There was no counter to that. That's why he was able to conquer Asia. In our day our scientific weaponry is the railroad, the telegraph, the rapid-fire gun, the smoke ordnance, and chlorine gas. It's all available now. It's a choice for the military leader whether to develop and use it. I made that decision where others didn't. I was the pioneer for more to follow. Other leaders will take up where I have left off and may do as well or better once they have studied in detail what we have done and how we did it. Genghis Khan did not devastate all the cities of Asia. He did not have to. His reputation and prowess were so great that Asia surrendered to his inevitability. He destroyed only the first cities that resisted. He piled up skulls outside of the first cities in nice, neat piles so that all could see what would happen to them if they resisted. That message got across the continent very quickly. The net result was that Genghis Khan ruled all of Asia with a force smaller in size than the army I currently command. The reader may wonder, does the general look upon himself as a Genghis Khan? And the answer is no, I am not that ambitious. My only ambition when this war was over was to go back out west, find my friend Gopan, sit at a campfire, smoke tobacco, and contemplate the Creator and the wonder of creation.

The logic of war is what military men study. Those who discover those laws of nature—the laws of war and how to abide by them—can become the greatest conquerors of history. It's that simple. Right now, because of the prowess of this army, no militia dared to stand up to it. And I would imagine that back east there were no Northern generals who wanted to volunteer to come out here and fight it. It was the Genghis Khan principle at work. Lincoln was thinking that he would smash Lee and Jackson first, seize Richmond, send the government out here to the west for protection, and then bring the full weight of the Northern army against us. But I knew Stonewall and Bobby Lee, as they now called them. They were nothing less than brilliant. They were the best military leaders on either side. I had faith that they would stop Lincoln's invasion of Virginia. When that happened, Lincoln would be in checkmate because he would not have enough time to raise another army to fight us out here and defend Washington at the same time.

The morning of June 14 came and went. We had managed to fully construct a new rail yard. This was the morning that I gave Forrest and his men the order to move his division up the line. His scouting patrols had been going up and down the track to Indianapolis all the last week. They reported that the enemy had made no effort to cut the line. No one in charge knew what our intentions were, but it was too late for them now anyway. Once Forrest moved up with his cavalry, the line would be securely ours.

Forrest's force covered the distance all the way to the target in three days, peeling companies off at bridges and vulnerable points. They encountered only irregulars and militia from the city of Indianapolis at the tail end of their journey. On the eighteenth, Forrest sent back word that the line was secure. I issued a warning order to Breckenridge to gather his corps at the rail assembly point in preparation for boarding the cars we had assembled at our new switching yard in Cincinnati.

On the morning of June 19, the corps was fully loaded along with their equipment. We had one hundred cars of all types, with horses in cattle cars, artillery pieces on flatbeds, and men in passenger cars and boxcars, a magnificent act of organization that the men themselves accomplished. I could take no credit whatsoever. These men wanted this war to end, and they wanted victory. I was but an instrument of their will. After a five-hour trip they started to offload and pour out of their trains. No real deployment into line of battle was necessary because there was no real opposing force that Forrest's men hadn't already swept out of the way. And much to my relief, there was no great conflagration this time. The men did see small fires break out in areas of the city that must have contained sensitive materials that the enemy did not want to fall into our hands. But for the most part, the city was a giant ghost town. Evidently, the traumatizing news of what had befallen Cincinnati a few weeks before had convinced most of the inhabitants to abandon their city a few weeks back.

Breckenridge assembled his corps onto a bivouac site on the evening of the nineteenth. On the twentieth they would stack arms, get out their hammers, irons, and salvage gear, and begin pulling up rails and loading the rails and whatever other equipment they could find onto the empty trains, to be sent south seeing that they would no longer need this material further north. They kept up with this work for several weeks, until nearly the end of July. They fanned out onto the other lines spider-webbed into the city, just as our men were doing to the lines going up to the other cities. Soon, all the major lines hooking up Chicago, St. Louis, Detroit, and Cleveland and all the little lines in between, with all the wheels, cars, and equipment, we had loaded up and sent south. Our foraging parties did similar work, sending back herds of hogs, cattle, and horses along with little livestock, chickens, seed corn, vegetables, and harvest. Along with the consumables also came machinery, whole steam engines, forges, factory and industrial equipment, and anything else that wasn't tied down solid.

Our parties went further and further into the Ohio breadbasket with each passing day. It seemed the people of the countryside were frozen with fear of what we would do to them if they didn't cooperate. Our first concern in June had been procuring livestock. But now as we got into mid- and late July, the emphasis shifted to taking produce from farms; we needed grains and vegetables as well as livestock. All surplus that the army didn't immediately need to consume went south. As long as we had train cars stocked with Confederate script, the system of procurement went better than expected. Richmond had not ordered us to pull out. They seemed happy with the constant flow of loot that we were sending. Along the way we even managed to liberate many banks of the content of their vaults and sent quite a sum of gold and silver coinage back to our cash-strapped government. With the much-needed iron rails and surplus railcars, this was becoming the world's first railroad and telegraph war. Sending men by rail kept them in such better shape than if they were tramping around in the dust in forced marches, which had been the norm until now. When they got to where they were going, they could put their energy into work rather than be spent on their feet.

Chapter 6

Sharpsburg/Antietam

The news back east had been exceptionally good. My hunch had been correct. Our superior generalship played out to the misfortune of the enemy. Jackson and Lee had driven the Army of the Potomac and their invasion all the way back to Harrison's Landing. The army of Lee had seriously repulsed them every step of the way, and their grand drive to Richmond miscarried. TJ had whipped several enemy armies in the Shenandoah with his little corps-sized force and then loaded trains to shuttle off to join Lee. One wondered how this could be. It was like a miracle. The Army of the Potomac was over twice the size of Lee's army.

The month of August went by quickly. Foraging and scrap operations continued. By the end of August, our army had gobbled up, cannibalized, rerouted, and reorganized nearly the entire enemy rail system heading to all the major cities. We heard that so many rails had piled up in Nashville that our people were diverting a portion of the surplus metal to the Confederate navy to nail onto the sides of steamships and turn them into ironclads—no more cotton-clad steamers. Our patrols and raiding parties had also fanned out to cut and procure every telegraph wire, and huge bales of the rolled-up wire started to pile up at all our bases. The Northern so-called Union was cut into two pieces, with one piece not able to adequately communicate with the other. The "Union" now, in all practicality, amounted to the industrial states of the Northeast, and that was it. The west was functioning apart from Washington's direct control.

The end of August saw the collapse of Lincoln's march on Richmond in the east. The Army of the Potomac finally abandoned the peninsula on the same barges that had brought them there. Then in northern Virginia, Lee, Longstreet, and Jackson smashed a large Northern army at Manassas Junction, a second but much more bloody battle there. I sensed, because I knew TJ and how he thought so well, that he would use this victory to convince whoever he had to that it was time for an invasion of the North. Lee would be of the same mind. They made a wonderful team, Jackson and Lee—I would say unbeatable, given the amazing victories they had achieved so far. It was a wonder to behold.

Things were developing rapidly back east, but we still had no orders from Richmond to change our position. I spent most of my days now poring over maps and scheming to get our army back into the fight. We had scouting parties, raiding parties, and foraging parties stretched out in all directions from our base for hundreds of miles. If Lee and Jackson were going to execute an invasion, then I would have to issue recall orders now if I were to get east in time to support them.

As far as where to strike, the answer was obvious. There was a rail line that went out from our base here all the way through southern Ohio, crossing over into West Virginia, Maryland, and finally, Baltimore. I'd had my eye on that line for weeks. I sent out scouts to watch over it, and they confirmed it was still intact. Evidently, Lincoln had never ordered it cut because it was the line over which he would need to rush an army out here to attack us. I thought he had lost this opportunity to try to dislodge us, before we got settled into our current positions, several weeks ago. Now we not only had a massive strike force but also had buttressed it with several state militias and irregular outfits that we had put all along our railroad network to protect it, thus keeping our strike force free to venture piecemeal by a series of reconnaissance-in-force penetrations ever farther north. My question was, wasn't there a single general who could advise Lincoln of his options and which opportunities to take and which ones to bypass? Evidently, there wasn't. It seemed that every opportunity that Lincoln had, his generals would squander. Both Lee and Jackson were fighting huge armies two or three times their size but were triumphant in kicking these forces out of the South. Something was terribly wrong in the Northern command structure. It never ceased to baffle me, but if it continued for another major battle, then it might be enough to put an end to this war. What good were the best-trained, best-equipped, best-fed soldiers on the planet if they didn't have generals who were smart enough to lead them?

I had made several inquiries and requests to move my army out over the last two weeks. I could feel it in my bones that the time for the knockout blow was at hand, before Lincoln could find a general to fight his war of aggression. But Richmond didn't want me to leave my base. I felt they were waiting on Lee to decide when he was going to invade the North. It would be logical for the invasion to take place on the heels of a great victory like the one that had just happened at Second Manassas. Then, on the last day of August, I got orders to support the Army of Northern Virginia, but with only half my army. The other half was to remain behind. Though somewhat frustrated with this splitting of the force, I decided to be happy with what I could get. Maybe half the force would be enough to deliver that knockout.

I issued recall orders on the first of September to various units associated with the half that would be moving out. It would take them at least one week to report in from all their scattered directions. I would be stripping this base of all of Forrest's cavalry, some 20,000 mounts. Normally, I would not think of taking away all of the cavalry, but I wanted this to be the last battle of the war, so I was going to do everything in my power to accomplish this, and cavalry was more useful in the pursuit, especially with a leader such as Forrest. By September 8, Forrest had his force ready, some 18,000 mounts. A few units were still out there, but we could not wait. The men and their animals were in good shape and had been well fed. They had kept active but were not worn out. They were in excellent physical shape for this battle, and morale couldn't be higher. On the eighth, Forrest gave the order to move out due east to secure the rail line all the way to Maryland.

On the tenth of September, I issued the order to assemble the men and their gear for boarding. The corps of Breckenridge and Polk would board the trains while the corps of Bragg and Hardee would stay here in reserve. I referred to their status as reserve because if I felt I needed them, I would issue orders for them and answer to Richmond later if need be. In the meantime, I wanted the men to be ready and alert to move immediately if necessary. I then did something that was uncharacteristic for me. I went out to all the remaining divisions and addressed them as a group at attention. I made it known to them all that I expected this to be the last battle of the war. If that proved true, then this might be the last time I would have the chance to talk to them as their commanding officer. I also told them that I had not addressed them as a group before primarily due to my Northern accent. I had always felt funny about it and didn't want any of them to feel uncomfortable about it. Anyhow, they all knew me very well by now. They knew my methods, but most of all, they knew my motivations and what was in my heart for them. I wanted to finish out this war so that they could go back to their families knowing that their nation, the Southern Nation, was safe and secure from any aggression. I promised them that the peace would be just and that they would no longer have anything to fear. I asked for their prayers and told them to be watchful for the good news that was about to coming their way. I was to move out with the striking force this time. Bragg was to be senior commander here.

It would be a five-hundred-mile train ride to the eastern theater. West would come east. We would attempt to make this ride in two days. Once we left base, we would not stop until arriving at the front. And God have mercy on whoever tried to get in the way. The morning of the twelfth arrived. We loaded all the trains with gear and equipment. All of the men were getting up out of their tents in the massive bivouac area outside of the train yard, where 150 cars lay stacked on switching tracks, ready to engorge themselves with Southern soldiery. Forrest had been out five days and no doubt had had several skirmishes with the enemy by now. We had a telegraph relay all the way to his position, and we were to scheduled to hear from him this morning to give us an all clear.

And then came what we had been waiting for, although not from Forrest. Richmond sent "hurry up and move out" orders. It looked like General Lee and I were on the same thought pattern. Evidently, he had decided to invade the North immediately upon the collapse of Lincoln's peninsula campaign, even before the victory at Manassas. Lee's army was presently in Maryland, having crossed the Potomac one week ago. This was stunning news.

We were all thrilled. This was shaping up to be another Shiloh. The frightening part was that Lee's force was not all that large, some 40,000, not even 50,000. But given Lee's performance at what they called the Seven Days and the beating he had given the Northerners at Manassas, maybe the magic would last. The whole situation mystified us, my staff and myself. By all accounts, the federal army—magnificently fed, equipped, and trained—faced disaster after disaster at the hands of a seriously under-strength ragtag army of walking skeletons, a ghost army. In contrast, my men had hardly stretched their legs or marched a fraction of what Lee and Jackson's army had been doing. I had them riding the rails now for every battle. And they'd gotten twice the clothing and three times the rations. They looked wonderful in their blue-dyed gray uniforms and their SN-buckled belts. When this war was over, if anyone came up to me and said, "There is the Alexander of the War Between the States," I would say, "How dare you say such a thing?" Lee and Jackson were the real Alexanders. But even so, I knew there were serious limits on what you could get out of an attacking army of 40,000 that was up against a defending army of over 100,000. At some point the laws of nature and war would kick in—no matter who was in command. Lee was taking a tremendous risk, and his army might come to annihilation just by a simple accident, like a mishandled order fallen into the hands of the enemy or an act of God. When I considered the incredible bravery of Lee, I could not help but weep with pride and fear for his safety.

My admiration for not just Jackson and Lee, but for every man and every officer in the eastern army, exploded in my mind and in my heart. They deserved a victory more than any other such group of men in history. What love and loyalty they must have for the Southern Nation to take such risks. Had any nation commanded such love and loyalty from its soldiers? We might have to go all the way back to Ancient Rome in order to find it. These men had taken outdated tactics and nonexistent resources and through pure willpower produced historic victories, one after another.

These victories were immortal but the product of mortal men. My victories, on the other hand, though strategically critical to the war, were less a triumph of the human spirit and more a simple trick of science. But I speak for myself and do not wish to take away anything from the enormous sacrifices of my men. They too performed brilliantly. Was I a general-in-chief of the Southern army in the traditional sense of the word or merely a handcuff magician who used modern contrivances to win battles, much like a magician uses bits of wire to pick locks? But my unorthodox methods of warfare coupled with the spiritual guidance I got from the spirit world together would be the key that unlocked the door to victory for the South.

But again, what about the Northern generals? Did they not go to the same military academy that I had attended? Did they not fight alongside of me in the Mexican War? Their only hope of victory was to drag the South into a war of attrition, but they so far had not been able to do that, even though it was the much simpler task.

At midmorning Forrest's message for the all clear came through. I issued the order—the army was to move out immediately. I summoned Bragg for a few last orders. I told him to gather his men in the assembly area after we had moved and to get them ready for a possible move. I told him to forget about salvage and foraging operations for the time being. He was to get his army ready. I told my staff that Lee had taken a great risk by invading the North with an undersized army and that it was our job to save him from possible annihilation. The situation could not be more grave than it was. One could not rely on the ineptitude of the

Northern generals forever. Speed was critical, but it could take as long as five days to cover the distance, assuming that the rail line was not sabotaged en route. I couldn't assume the same kind of naïveté that the Northern forces out here had been guilty of, having hardly pulled up a rail in defense of their cities. And that we were now a rail-born army was no secret anymore either. They knew how we would be coming. We might find ourselves in a pitched battle upon arrival. The lead train would have a flatbed with four Gatling guns at the ready and several cattle cars full of tools and crews ready to put back rails or repair damaged bridges. The departure time was noon, September 12, 1862.

A courier detachment from General Forrest arrived in the late morning to confirm that all the bridges were secure all the way to Martinsburg, Maryland. The enemy had cut telegraph wires in several places and had dug up several stretches of rail line. Some, Forrest's men had been able to put back together. Others, our crews would have to repair. We took along several flatbed loads of rails to replace anything we came across along the way. Forrest had detached companies all along the five-hundred-mile route to guard bridges and passes. He had stretched his resources razor-thin, and we would have to relieve these detachments quickly so that they would have enough time to regroup at the front and take part in the great battle that we knew was waiting to greet us when we all got there. The couriers told us that we would have trouble at the two bridge crossings over the northern and southern branches of the Potomac. Forrest had been successful in driving the guard mounts off of the two bridges, but there was a straightaway section in between where the rails were torn up and the rails themselves impossible to salvage. I estimated that repairs to the line would cost us a day in travel, which wasn't bad.

Noontime arrived finally. Trains were full. One after another, the locomotives pulled out of the switching yard. Unfortunately, men had to ride on the roofs again, but it turned out that some enjoyed being in the open air, and there was no shortage of volunteers. I was hoping we could get twenty miles per hour during the day and fifteen at night. The Northern tracks were of a higher quality, and the Northern engineers had maintained them much better than we were used to in the South. Many of our trains, we had accumulated through seizure, courtesy of our hosts in Ohio and Indiana. I ordered the lead trains to push the equipment as they could. We managed to get twenty-five miles per hour as top speed on straightaways, of which there were many. We started running into the detachments of Forrest's cavalry on the night of the fourteenth on the boundary into western Virginia.

The morning of the fifteenth came, and the trains were still moving along clear tracks. We had passed over three spots that Forrest's men had put back together after the enemy had hastily torn them up. By noon on the fifteenth, we had crossed the North Potomac on the Maryland border and met up with Forrest and the long stretch of torn-up track. Forrest told us that Jackson's army had been through Martinsburg three days ago to drive the Union forces out toward a showdown at Harper's Ferry. The eastern army was split, with Jackson's force going after Harper's Ferry and

Lee's force concentrated at Sharpsburg on Antietam Creek, where Lee was determined to make a stand.

Forrest mentioned to me that we could unload here and march the rest of the way. But I decided to have our repair crews fix the gap so that we could take the trains down to Martinsburg courtesy of the Baltimore and Ohio Railroad. The men frantically threw themselves into the work of reinstalling rail ties and hammering in rails. The work gangs worked in relays. The crews would hustle up rails, fit them on the ties, and hammer them into place at the double-quick until they were completely out of breath. Once the men started to falter, the next relay would come in. The intervals were around twenty minutes. The crews had closed the gap by sundown. In the meantime, the men had refueled the locomotives, and steam was up. The trains went in motion once again.

Forrest's cavalry was two-thirds regrouped and had been pushing ahead of the trains throughout the night. At sunrise on the sixteenth, the trains pulled into Martinsburg. Disembarkation began at 6:30 a.m. By noon the two corps of the Army of the West had fully unloaded the trains. The corps began to form up into units in echelon for the march to the front.

Forrest sent couriers forward from his staff to locate General Lee and tell him of the arrival of the Army of the West. In the early afternoon we allowed the men to stand down and take rations for what could be their last time before engaging the enemy. Forrest's couriers contacted Lee's headquarters on the Antietam at about 6:00 p.m. on September 16. I was tempted to put the army in motion and march toward the Antietam during the night without orders. But I decided to let the men bivouac for the night and wait for orders. Couriers came back after midnight. Lee would engage with the enemy on the seventeenth at his current position. We were to get on the road as soon as practicable to join the battle from the west.

The order to strike the tents and move out would go out at 3:00 a.m. In the meantime, I spent my time going over maps, finding roads and prospective assembly areas where we could put the army of 50,000 on line. The most direct route was the road from Martinsburg to Shepardstown and then the road due east into Sharpsburg. From the hasty map that the couriers had drawn up, that would put the Army of the West smack in the middle of the battlefield. At 3:00 a.m. the officers rousted the sergeants, who in turn woke up the men. By sunrise the men were already on the road. Six thousand of Forrest's mounts were in the vanguard. They would be the first to reach the battlefield and would represent a powerful mobile first punch. At two hours into the march, we could hear far-off cannon fire. It started as a distant, faint groaning from the east. Gradually, it grew. By eleven o'clock we had cleared Shepardstown, and the noise level held constant. By 3:30 p.m. Breckenridge's corps was on the outskirts of Sharpsburg at Lee's headquarters. I rode up to the commander to offer our services.

"General Worth, thank God you have arrived," said General Lee. "The army is in a precarious position at the moment. Our weakest point is in the center. We are able to hold these positions at present, but all our reserves are committed. I am depending on A. P. Hill's division, which is still on its way from Harper's Ferry, to relieve the pressure on my right when it gets here, but our position at this time is strictly defensive."

"General Lee, have no fear. Behind me I have two full corps stretched out all the way to Shepardstown, and I will be feeding them into the battle as they arrive. Our corps and cavalry division will provide you all the offensive punch you need to win this battle. If I might be so bold, sir, why don't you let us come in and initiate the offense while you observe and rest your men? We know what to do and are itching to do it."

"General Worth, I have the utmost respect for your accomplishments out west and give you my full authority right now to attack the enemy and drive them from this field."

With that I saluted the white-haired legend and turned to my artillery chiefs. "Bring forward your artillery batteries and lay as much smoke as possible east of Middle Bridge. Leave the bridge and the area beyond it clear so we can deploy our corps."

Within twenty minutes several dozen pieces had clamored through the town. They unlimbered and started pouring smoke ordnance in a huge masking operation. Meanwhile, regiment after regiment moved at a double-quick up the Boonsboro Road through the center of town and stayed in file toward the bridge. We flanked them with twenty Gatling guns, ten per side. Once Breckenridge's corps was across the bridge, the guns would go into the vanguard position to smash up the enemy formation. There were two enemy corps immediately across the bridge, Porter's Fifth

Corps and Sumner's Second, and in addition, Burnside's Ninth Corps had been trying to deploy over Lower Bridge all day. For the moment we would leave the counterattack on the Ninth up to A. P. Hill's division, assuming it arrived as General Lee had assured us it would. My plan was to get both of my corps across Middle Bridge and launch an immediate attack. With sunlight now at a premium, if we could get in two good hours of attacking, we could smash their line and at least drive them off of this field before sundown. From all reports I had gathered within the hour, the fighting had been grueling and ferocious all day. The two corps we faced were shattered. Casualties were staggering. We saw some horrific, ghastly sights as we passed by a sunken road, later to be known as the Bloody Lane. This was an area to be covered by remnants of General D. H. Hill's division.

At 4:30 p.m. Breckenridge's corps crossed Middle Bridge unmolested, artillery cloaked by a thick curtain of smoke to the east. How fast could 20,000 men double-quick over a bridge? That was a question we had answered by 4:15 p.m.: at a rate of about 1,200 per minute. The cavalry had already found fords across the creek. Our men didn't have to go dry-shod, but since no one was challenging their passage over the bridge, we kept them going. Polk's corps was right behind. But first we needed to get the firepower across. This included ten Gatling guns and twenty cannons.

By 5:00 p.m., Breckenridge ordered his men, now on line of battle, onto the attack. Syke's division was dug in at a hasty position west of Porterstown. They were the ripe fruit that Breckenridge's men had to harvest. Instead of the usual cumbersome artillery barrage, ten Gatling guns opened fire and raked the enemy line with rapid fire. Our cannons focused on counter-battery fire to protect the Gatling guns. We had two cannons assigned to every gun in support. No Gatling guns took a hit. After twenty minutes of constant strafing, Syke's division got themselves up off the ground and ran anywhere they could to escape—they simply melted away in a skedaddle. We never knew for sure if they had suffered from an unusual rate of casualties or if they had became totally demoralized by feelings of powerlessness due to the violence of the attack and the volume of lead that our crews were firing in their direction. Our men were not receiving much shot in their direction in return. The Union soldiers were a spent force and had lost the initiative. There was a thickly wooded area beyond Peterstown, and the blue forms our scouts were seeing were all heading in that direction.

It was 5:30 p.m., and there was a half hour to go before sunset. A. P. Hill's division had made it as Lee had said and was driving Burnside's men across Lower Bridge. With the limited time left in the day, I ordered one last push—a left wheel for the corps and a charge for Forrest's cavalry, hopefully to roll up the enemy left flank. A scout report led us to believe we were heading directly for McClellan's headquarters and McClellan himself. He was holding two divisions in reserve, but one was too far off in the distance to come to his defense. The other one was behind him, putting him between us and the division. He was totally exposed to our assault. He had no doubt witnessed the crumbling of Syke's division but dithered on how to counter it. When

Forrest and his cavalry bore down on the commander's tent, they were met with a white flag. The commander of the Army of the Potomac had surrendered. Shortly afterward, Breckenridge's corps had completed its left wheel maneuver and now stood in a line of battle to which there was no counter, situated in front of McClellan's headquarters. Polk's corps had just completed its bridge crossing and also executed a left wheel before sundown. The Army of the West was now fully across Antietam Creek and presented the enemy with a view of a massive sea of gray.

I sent members of my staff back across Middle Bridge as fast as they could ride to give General Lee the word that we were in the process of taking the commander of the Army of the Potomac prisoner. Fighting was still going on to our south. At 6:15 p.m., I sent word to McClellan that he must order an immediate ceasefire to all of his corps and division commanders. It was merciful to all that the evening's twilight put an end to all fighting and gave time for word of the surrender to spread.

The men were to hold their positions and sleep on their arms this night of the seventeenth. Wagons with rations trickled up the line. Campfires appeared all over the field, and the men on both sides started to grasp the reality that the war was over. The officers had to warn their men to keep down the exhilaration since the details and formalities of the surrender had yet to totally manifest.

General Forrest was the first to make direct contact with General McClellan at the latter's headquarters. I sent word to Forrest to confirm that McClellan had issued orders to his army to stand down and stack their arms. He was then to accept the general's sword, take him into custody, and proceed to General Lee's position. In the morning we would start the process of disarming and paroling the Army of the Potomac, something with which our army had now had much practice. The confiscation of the Army of the Potomac's supply trains would also begin.

In the whirlwind of the day, we had gotten to observe the condition of our comrades in the Army of Northern Virginia only from a distance. But they were a sorry sight to behold, underfed, overmarched, shoeless, and dressed in rags. Those lads didn't look like they'd had a square meal in six months. That would all change now. They would be at the front of the line for all that we could get for them. I would make sure those rope belts and rope suspenders were the first things to go. From what I had in a short time observed among the eastern army, I could see clearly that those Southern gentlemen in Richmond, through either hubris or neglect, had never conceived of an adequate plan to feed and equip the armies of the South. In their rush to war, coming up with a workable plan of logistics had been an afterthought, but our men from the west would show them how to live now in spite of everything. It would all start with turning those Union belts upside down. The next several days would be ones of feeding, delousing, and discarding unserviceable clothing and equipment for the whole of Lee's army. My men were to show them how.

Chapter 7

Lincoln

On the eighteenth of September, Lee summoned the generals and his staff for a council of war, which now was instead a council of peace. The surrender of McClellan started a process of negotiating peace terms with Lincoln. We had several issues to consider. Were we to leave the diplomacy to Richmond, or were we to act together as a military government to execute the terms? I made my opinions known to the generals. Given that the war didn't have to be fought in the first place but had been a massive failure of diplomacy from the beginning, I felt that Richmond had forfeited its prerogative and would botch the peace.

"With the high-mindedness of the Richmond government, they will make lasting peace impossible," I said, "and we will have to fight this war over again in the coming years. And then there is the issue of slavery. Lincoln and the Republicans will never let this issue go away. If we don't come up with a solution among ourselves to solve this issue, Lincoln will simply come back from a six-month truce to raise more armies and take another shot at us, even if he has to move the capital all the way up to the Canadian border. He has been fighting this war with one arm tied behind his back. According to our estimates of available military-aged men in the North, all he has to do is bring that other arm out from behind his back and wallop us with it. We, on the other hand, can't feed the armies we have and at present are operating way beyond our available resources."

General Lee listened to me with a stern look on his face and in his eyes. "General Worth, I do see the logic behind your analysis of the situation all too clearly. This war is an abomination to Almighty God, but it has been our duty to fight it. I have no doubt that Lincoln will continue to fight this war if he does not achieve his moral aims. And in all candidness, it is no longer practicable in this day to fight a war in defense of the institution of slavery. Generals Jackson, Longstreet, and I, along with many other officers in our commands and staffs, have come to the conclusion that it is not consistent with our Christian beliefs to maintain this institution any longer. As the officer in charge of this council, I order you to go to Washington and speak with the leader of the government there on the appropriate terms of peace. I will not declare our military council to be a military government, however. We will still bow to the wishes of the civilian government in Richmond, with the provision that most of the officers in my command, all the corps and division officers, most of the line officers, and I myself will submit our resignations in the event that Richmond decides to take over the peace negotiations. With this order you have my full authority and support."

With that pronouncement, the council ended. Because time was now critical, I wasted none of it. I sent members of my staff over to the former headquarters of McClellan and established contact with Washington for a meeting with President Lincoln just as fast as we could arrange it. I now had a diplomatic war on my hands. My plan was to cut a deal with Lincoln hard and fast and bring it back here to Lee, who would then present it to Richmond as a fait accompli. The government at Richmond, now renowned for its tardiness and ineptitude, would have to either accept the deal or face mass resignations among the officer corps in the army, to include all of its most talented leaders.

We made contact with the authorities in Washington that afternoon of the nineteenth. On the morning of the twentieth, my staff and I were to board a train in Martinsburg that would take us all the way into Washington that day. I had requested a meeting with President Lincoln that evening. We also had a security detachment with us.

On the evening of the twentieth, we went by coach into the city itself. It was nothing like I had remembered it from my boyhood. The war had transformed it. It was now a giant military base studded with ominous-looking forts with heavy guns. *The time to end this war is now*, I thought. Finally, the ride ended at the White House, where I was greeted by Major General Henry Halleck. We did not exchange any pleasantries. I was sure he hated the sight of me, considered me a traitor, and wondered why a good New York boy like me was representing the group of rebels that was dissolving the country.

"Good evening, General Worth. Please follow me," he said tersely.

I followed him to a side room at the end of a long hallway.

"The president is waiting for you in here."

I entered the room, and sitting at a desk was the rail-splitter himself. He stood up and offered his hand. "Good evening, General."

"Good evening, sir."

"We sent you all the way to Texas, and you have fought your way back here like an avenging god of war. We obviously trained you too well."

"Mr. President, I fought alongside many Southerners during the Mexican War, where I received much of my practical training. I owed several of them my life and could not wield my sword against them in anger. This war was a tragic mistake that I hope may end today."

"Yes, it was a mistake, but the biggest mistake was all of the talented officers like you who went for the South. My mistake was fighting a war without a single general officer capable of winning a battle. And this mistake has brought us here today."

"Nevertheless, sir, I am here with the authority to grant a peaceful end to this war and an end to the further loss of your Northern cities."

"Yes, you do have a point," said Lincoln. "My government right now is like a hog-tied sow with all the teats exposed for milking." With that, he picked up a paper from the desk and walked it over to a fireplace, where the embers were still aglow. He appeared ready to throw the paper into the fire.

"Can I ask you what is on that paper, sir?"

"Certainly," Lincoln said. "It was my Proclamation of Emancipation of the Southern slaves. I was going to issue it formally after we had won this battle of Antietam. But now that we have lost, I shall toss it into the flames."

"Now hold on a second, sir. Can I read that?"

"Sure, you can have it as a souvenir."

I quickly scanned past all the legal jargon to find the crux. "Mr. President, how did this come about? Did you write this document?"

"No, I provided all the legal wording, but the idea of it came to me through a friend of my wife and me, little Nettie."

"Little Nettie?" I asked.

"Yes, Nettie Coburn. She is a spiritualist medium who comes here to do séances. You see, General, I have become a spiritualist. I would appreciate it if you could please keep this to yourself. Are you familiar with the religion of spiritualism?"

"As a matter of fact, Mr. President, not only am I familiar with it, but I also consider myself one—although my path to the religion has come through contact with Indian medicine men who are the same as the so-called mediums like the Fox sisters that I have read about in the New York newspapers. I have kept track of the Fox sisters and their movement and assume this Nettie Coburn is from the same group?"

"My wife is more familiar with the different people associated with the religion. They are also mixed in with the abolitionists. Many are from both groups. Well, what a coincidence, General, that we should be members of the same religion in a roundabout way. Quite ironic. But it seems that little Nettie's predictions regarding this proclamation have fallen short of the mark. Her spirit guides told her that this document would lead to freedom for the slaves. However, we have lost this war to you and the slaveholders, so I don't see how this piece of paper serves any further purpose other than kindling. And this leads me to ask a question of you, General. If you and I are truly both of the same beliefs, then how is it you stand here representing the interests of the slaveholders? Do you not also believe that all human beings possess the divine spark of the infinite within them and are entitled to live in freedom under nature's laws?"

"Mr. President, thank you for bringing our discussion to the point so quickly. Evidently, there is much you don't know about the Southern mentality and the desires of the Southern people. Let me enlighten you regarding what my mission is as their representative. First of all, I do not represent the interests of the plantation owners and slaveholders, and neither does the Southern Army. We represent the Southern people and the Southern way of life. It was the moneyed class and, if I may say so, the government of the United States with its cotton tariffs that transformed the genteel, laid-back, courteous society into the monstrous creation it became, with the exploitation of the slave folk to satisfy the greed of that moneyed class and fill the coffers of the Department of the Treasury. You and I can fix that today. Southerners looked upon slavery in a nostalgic, naive way where both slaves and slave owners were supposed to find mutual benefit. This, of course, was an erroneous illusion that the invention of the cotton gin made only too clear to us. But let's talk about right now. In exchange for your formal recognition of the government of the Southern Nation, war reparations, and reparations for the purchase of freedom for the slaves, I am authorized to offer in return complete emancipation of the slaves, in agreement with this document of yours that you were about to discard."

Lincoln looked upon me with total disbelief. "I am quite taken aback by this, General. This is quite unexpected. Do you really think that Mr. Davis will abolish slavery? Who has given you this authorization to make this offer? It's written right into your constitution, Article 1, Section 9, that there will be no law denying the right to own slaves, and in Article 4, Section 3, all new territory acquired by the Confederacy is to have slavery. Are you telling me that the government in Richmond is going to rewrite its constitution? I don't believe it!"

"Mr. President," I said, "what Richmond wants or has wanted in the past is irrelevant now in light of current events. The war council of General Robert E. Lee and the officer corps of the Southern Army have deemed it a military necessity and imperative to national security that we abolish slavery. My authorization to make the offer comes from them. If the politicians in Richmond don't agree, then there will be wholesale resignations of virtually the entire officer corps of the South, including myself. Richmond will be on its own. They can't afford this. The government could not survive in this case. But we do insist on having financial compensation for the slaveholders as a condition for emancipation. This, we feel, is our right since the United States government has profited off of slavery for years. We will need this guarantee to silence opposition to the plan. It will enable us to put the past behind us in all respects. We also demand money to compensate the slaves themselves, especially those engaged in the cotton industry. It's only fair, and if you agree to this, then the war will be over. If you are not willing to come to an agreement today, then General Lee's council may decide to carry on with the war. Let me remind you that we still have a substantial western army waiting for orders to go further north and take more of your cities, and as of now you have no army to protect them. I would require a substantial down payment in gold bullion that we could pick up in a few days as a gesture of your commitment to our terms."

"But what about your principles, General? Do you not believe that all human beings have the right to be free?"

"Of course, I do, Mr. President. But I also believe in the law of cause and effect. You can't expect the people of the South to absorb all of the responsibility, moral and otherwise, and just free the slaves willy-nilly without compensation when a good half of the responsibility lies with the North, which has also benefited from all the inhumane exploitation over the decades. I see myself fighting for the freedom of the slaves just as much as you. And I have little sympathy for the Northern government's situation right now. You would not let the states secede but instead precipitated this catastrophic war. Your gamble has failed. And if losing half the country and compensation is the price you have to pay, then let it be a lesson for all future governments. Whatever religion you may be, the law of nature is supreme."

"I must say that this discussion has surprised me. I never

expected the terms that you are offering. I regret that this conversation couldn't have taken place years ago, before my presidency, when the whole notion of secession and war was not an issue. Then we could still be one nation instead of two. But it was not God's will. Yet we can still make the best of the new situation. Very well then. We may have to borrow the money, but you will have your compensation and your recognition. And I will have what little Nettie's guides promised me, but I never expected it to happen this way."

"Mr. President, I need to return with this agreement in writing, a signed statement of what we have agreed to. You, sir, are the lawyer. I would request that you write it in the form of a legally enforceable treaty."

"Very well, General. Let's put this war behind us." With that the president called in witnesses and drew up a document of terms. These terms included the immediate cessation of hostilities, compensation, reparations for slaveholders and slaves, reparations to the Southern military in the form of rations and supplies for the duration of the withdrawal from Northern territory over a period of six months, and a declaration of permanent peace and friendship, to be signed by the representatives of both countries after six months. I signed the document on behalf of General Lee.

I traveled back to Martinsburg the next day, document in hand, and presented it to General Lee. For the first time since the Mexican War, I saw a grin come across his face.

"I knew you would be able to reason with those people," he said. "After all, you were born among them and knew their ways far better than any of us. The people of the South owe you their existence as a free and independent nation. You have done so much good for us. God bless you, General!" Then something happened that was totally uncharacteristic, or so you would think for a front commander. A tear of joy streamed down his face. I suspect that it was not the tear of a front commander but the tear of a father who had three sons serving in uniform. It was a tear of joy for them with the knowledge that they would not have to die in this dreadful war—that they would live and bring Lee many grandchildren.

I left it up to Lee, Jackson, and all the other officers to make their cases for the agreement to the Richmond government. But after much drama, haggling, and hand-wringing with the politicians at Richmond for several weeks after the great victory, the pious General Jackson, no doubt with God's angels standing on either side to encourage him, with his deep blue eyes lit up, gave a most eloquent sermon on the need for and righteousness of emancipation. "Let the blood of our brave dead wash our souls clean of our national sins as the blood of Christ has redeemed us of our personal sins and allowed us residence in the heavenly kingdom," he said, or something to that effect. The force of Lee's personality and logic made Davis and the other Southern gentlemen swallow their pride for once in their lives and agree that what we had worked out was the only feasible path and the only possible foundation on which to build our Southern Nation. We would become a people, a culture, and whole once again.

As for myself, once the six-month withdrawal phase from Northern territory was over, I requested and received a post back to the place that I loved—sweet Texas! From there I met up once again with my old friends in Arizona, the Apaches, Gopan, and others. I did not seek notoriety but wished only to be left alone in the land where my father had last walked the earth. There I would resume my old army assignment, smoke tobacco, talk to my friends, and contemplate the greatness of the Creator.